THE BRIDESMAN

Savyon Liebrecht

THE BRIDESMAN

*Translated from the Hebrew
by Gilah Kahn-Hoffmann*

Europa
editions

Europa Editions
27 Union Square West, Suite 302
New York NY 10003
www.europaeditions.com
info@europaeditions.com

Translation by Gilah Kahn-Hoffmann
Original title: *HaShoshbin*
Translation copyright © 2023 by Savyon Liebrecht

Library of Congress Cataloging in Publication Data is available
ISBN 978-1-60945-997-0

Liebrecht, Savyon
The Bridesman

Art direction by Emanuele Ragnisco
instagram.com/emanueleragnisco

Cover image: Douglas Volk, *After the Reception*,
oil on canvas, 1887

Cover design by Ginevra Rapisardi

Prepress by Grafica Punto Print – Rome

Printed in Canada

CONTENTS

THE BRIDESMAN

PART ONE
ADELLA

Twenty-four years after I left Israel, Adella invited me to cross the ocean. Did she do it just so I could write her life story?

By then I was already a seasoned ghostwriter, intimately familiar with the secret games of deception people are so extraordinarily adept at playing with their memories. And yet, in all the books I wrote—especially for those clients who had reached a grand old age, some of them famous—the details of the tale were dependent upon what they told me, and if they chose to create a new life story for themselves, there was no way I could distinguish between fact and fabrication.

But I knew Adella from childhood, and this was the first time that I could straddle the gap between the facts as I knew them and the way they were perceived by others. Things I saw in her with my own eyes as a boy were revealed to me now as I looked back, and I was astonished: sparks that were hidden within her then, how they were able to extinguish themselves and die, and how, like a dormant volcano reawakening, they could erupt and demolish their surroundings.

I was nine when I met her for the first time, on a Saturday evening in the winter that would be recorded as the rainiest of the decade. She sat on the green velvet armchair in my grandfather's spacious living room, folded deep into its recesses as though seeking shelter from the many pairs of prying eyes boring into her, and from the men and women—my aunts and uncles—who approached and studied her face and body, standing in front of her and shamelessly scrutinizing the girl from the top of her drenched head, to her eyes, scarily magnified behind the thick lenses of her glasses, down to the soles of her feet, which dangled in the air, shifting their gaze back to the hair plastered to her scalp as though doused by a bucket of water, to the drops of rain that she hadn't managed to wipe away with the handkerchief she held so that they slid from her glasses along her neck, wetting her shirt. And then the adults went back to their chairs, scowling as if they had no idea whether or not she was suitable, most of them summarily dismissing her as they reinserted themselves into the flowing conversation in Hebrew, peppered with Farsi words and expressions, about gossip and business affairs.

I didn't know then that she had made up her mind to marry my uncle even before she laid eyes on him. That if she didn't, she would be forced by her aunts to marry the old man, his mouth crowded with teeth, who seemed to be perpetually grinning and was always lying in wait for her outside the boarding school.

I sat at the adults' table next to my mother. My brother Rafi was serving in the army, my sister Yarden was busy studying for her matriculation exams, and neither of them was willing to come with us. Usually the children were sent into the next room to watch television and weren't allowed to sit with the adults until it was time to serve the savory pastries and the cakes. These were preceded by a hearty meal that always included rice and sometimes fish or fried zucchini. At the end of the table stood the traditional *hamin*, which had simmered overnight, and in our family was made with turkey necks and red beans, which almost no one sampled, and was the mainstay of my grandfather's and my uncle's meals for the rest of the week. But my status was different from that of the other children ever since my father had left for Los Angeles and my mother had stopped smiling. Suddenly I was the recipient of caresses and compassionate looks from my uncles and aunts. Esther, my mother's sister, would gather me into her fragrant bosom every time we met, and my grandfather would secretly cram double the usual allowance into my pocket.

And so I sat with the grownups on that wintry evening, slightly hidden behind the bulk of Uncle Yosef, and observed Adella, whose name I had yet to learn, fascinated by the way she kept wiping the lenses of her owlish glasses, putting them back on and casting sideways glances at the people in the room. I tugged at my mother's sleeve and asked, tilting my chin toward the guest, "Who's that?" and she shushed me with a "Not now."

My mother had four brothers and three sisters, and they would all come to my grandfather's house every week—all of them except for the third brother, Mordechai, the Jerusalemite, who had stopped being religiously observant. This time, in honor of the special event, he came too, and didn't spare my aunts his well-known opinion of them: "You are a bunch of two-faced domineering females. At least my wife went to school and now she's a teacher, but you—not one of you is educated or works outside the home, even though you are no less talented than the men in the family."

These gatherings took place every Saturday evening, af-ter Shabbat. The velvet tablecloth embroidered with peacock feathers stitched by my grandmother was spread over the large dining-room table. My saintly grandmother, who died the death of a righteous person on the holy Jewish day of Yom Kippur, and had an uncanny talent for finding the rare black pomegran-ates said to cure disease when the family lived by the market in Tehran. At the head of the table sat Uncle Yosef, the eldest son, who owned a clothing store. For as long as I can remember I had always tried to dodge Uncle Yosef. Even when his hand was outstretched in an apparent desire to bestow a fond pat, if the pudgy fingers managed to snare my nose, he would pinch it so hard that it would smart for long moments, red and tingling.

His brother Menashe, who owned a bakery, always sat

beside him as if awaiting his orders, as he had done ever since they were children.

The fourth brother, Moshe, was the only bachelor in the family, the handsomest of the brothers and the favorite of the children. He never raised his voice to us and never made any demands. He would cradle the babies in his arms and coo at them until they smiled, and when they grew up and he didn't know what to say to them he would hide his trembling hands under the table and grin broadly, beaming his love to them in that way.

My mother's three sisters were scattered around the table, two of them next to their husbands and one sitting on her own—Vika, Esther, and Lily—in their birth order. It was as if my late grandmother was also with us at the table, for every so often the siblings would absent-mindedly brush their fingers across one of the embroidered feathers, to conjure a memory of their mother's presence.

Suddenly my Aunt Vika, my mother's eldest sister, stood up, and with a barely perceptible jerk of her head, which didn't bode well, indicated the adjacent room. My other two aunts jumped to their feet and followed her, while my mother dawdled deliberately until they had disappeared into the room, and only then, as though making up her own mind to go and not because she had been told to do so, did she join them, pulling me along behind her.

Sometimes my mother and her sisters would have the most wonderful times together, embracing one another for no apparent reason, weeping real tears over each other's heartache, laughing till they were gasping, telling stories about how the family had arrived from Iran thirty-five years before, in 1950, and how the synagogue in the Old City of Jerusalem collapsed owing to an unusually violent storm. And sometimes an unyielding silence reigned, as if they were enemies from birth, and even the fact that they sat together in the women's section at the synagogue to mark the new moon and the new month and recited the *Ya'aleh Ve'yavo* prayer, beseeching God to treat them with compassion and loving-kindness, was of no avail.

The moment that the door to my grandfather's bedroom closed, I could feel the agitation. Vika began inundating the terrified Lily with questions, and as she considered her responses her practiced hands smoothed out the bedspread and plumped up the pillows.

And there, in words vague and straightforward, elusive and direct, the provenance of the young guest became clear to me, that she was one of the students at the boarding school where my cousin Rina, Lily's daughter, was a teacher.

Once a week, when Rina worked the nightshift, her mother would bring her special dishes that didn't upset her delicate stomach, and in that way she had become familiar with the boarding school and the girls who lived there.

"You said that she's one of us." Vika fired her opening shot.

"One of us, of course."

"She doesn't know that for us wearing a purple skirt the first time you meet someone is bad luck?"

"That's not a Persian custom, it's our family custom—there's a difference. Not to mention, how should she know? She grew up without a mother from age ten."

"Does she observe Shabbat?" Vika ignored the answer.

"Of course she does."

"So how did she get here today from Givat Ada without leaving before Shabbat was over? She flew through the air?"

"Who said she came from Givat Ada? She spent Shabbat at the house of her friend from the boarding school. She lives in the neighborhood on Hahistadrut Street, it's a ten-minute walk from here."

Vika was silent. It seemed that she had received an answer to each of her questions.

"You said she's eighteen." She seemed to have run out of questions.

"She's eighteen, of course."

"She looks older."

"Because of the glasses. Rina has been teaching her since ninth grade. She's eighteen. Stop looking for things. And besides, Ima came to me in a dream."

"What about family; does she have any?" Vika ignored the last comment about their mother. In a dream.

"Her father took off when she was a baby, and her mother, who remained bound to him without a divorce, died when the girl was ten."

"And what about the aunts?"

"All of a sudden they want to marry her off to someone, but when she was ten, no one wanted her. They packed her off to a boarding school."

"Because of the foot?"

"Because they have no heart."

On a certain level, each of them knew deep down—even I understood it as a boy—that the girl being an orphan worked in the family's favor; no one would object that an eighteen-year-old girl was being married to a disabled thirty-eight-year-old, and no one would be asking any questions about him. Alone in the world, except for her aunts who couldn't care less about her welfare, she would be glad to have a family and a roof over her head, and since the world hadn't exactly showered her with affection, she would be grateful for any small kindness.

"What does she do at the boarding school?"

"What do you think they do at a boarding school?"

"Go on, tell us, and then maybe we'll be as clever as you are." Vika imitated the mocking tone used by the men in the family as she repeated the sentence that they routinely used to belittle the women.

Cowed as she was, it seemed that she had reached the end of

her rope, and first and foremost Lily shocked herself with her sudden shriek.

"What do you want from me?" the screech that issued from Lily's throat was like no sound her sisters had ever heard her make before. "In the entire boarding school she's the only Persian girl. She does her homework and gets good grades, knows how to sew and to knit and to cook. And even Ima said in the dream that a poor orphan will be a good wife for Moshe. What do you want from my life, interrogating me as if I had brought a murderer into the house?"

Lily's screams and the repeated references to their mother who had appeared in a dream seemed to dampen Vika's fighting spirit. All she said was, "And you didn't notice that she limps and she's probably legally blind?" Not bothering to wait for a reply, arranging her features to convey that she had won this battle, she opened the door, strode defiantly over to where the men were gathered, pulled out a chair and joined them. One by one her sisters returned to the table, where they closed ranks and spoke in voices high-pitched and low. My mother made space for me beside her and pulled me close, and I sat pressed against her thigh, inhaling the scent of the shampoo that she kept in a small bottle in the medicine cabinet. So that's how it was. This young girl, who was alone in the world and from the age of ten had grown up in an orphanage like Oliver Twist, was intended, despite her aunts, and with the help of my grandmother who came in a dream, to be Uncle Moshe's bride.

I saw her in a new light, suddenly aware of the beauty of her face. Soon she would be my aunt, the wife of my favorite uncle. She was still ensconced in the armchair, but now she was seated with her head inclined and her expression had changed. Her eyes, which had previously darted to the sides or been downcast against the onslaught of her inquisitors, were now open wide and glittering behind the lenses of her glasses, slowly wandering over the new, old-style furniture and the framed needlepoints hanging on the wall in rows, like stamps in an album. Her hair had fluffed up as it began to dry, revealing its light color and framing her face in a flattering way. My gaze travelled to her legs, whose weakness my mother had mentioned, and I could clearly see that one was shorter than the other and that the shorter leg was thinner and hanging loosely, the toes pointing inward inside the wet shoe.

It seemed she was relieved that people were no longer concerned with her and were now sitting and conversing among themselves, reaching occasionally for the refreshments arrayed on the table in small dishes, shifting from left to right and thus providing her with fleeting glimpses of the groom. Despite her poor eyesight, perhaps she could discern the outline of his attractive head, his straight white teeth. And he, sitting at a distance of two seats away, dared to raise his head and look over at her from time to time. What he thought was hard to tell from his frozen features, but for quite a while the two potentially betrothed individuals sat at opposite ends of the room, stealing glances at each other.

Surrounded by my uncles and aunts, vaguely aware of the recording of the Weekly Portion of the Torah recounting how the Lord forgave the Israelite assembly He brought out of Egypt for doubting Him, which my grandfather liked to play in a loop in the weeks leading up to Yom Kippur, hearing the shouts and laughter from my cousins in the next room, I was flooded with the sense of strength which derived from the enveloping presence of my large family, and it seemed palpable to me, a warm, all-encompassing wave which held us in its embrace and wordlessly assured our abiding connection. Even the arguments which occasionally broke out around the table or the harsh words which were sometimes uttered, usually criticism about the way someone's children were being raised, and even the periods of enraged silence which lasted until one of the siblings intervened and coaxed the antagonists to make amends, none of these dulled for a moment the unwavering confidence in the power of the family—a safety net spun of steel struts and love—always cradled below me, in everlasting support. My cousins, whom I loved with all my heart, even the ones who picked on me for being so attached to my mother and because my nose was always in a book, were my Dream Team. I was ready to throw myself under a bus for any one of them, to die for the people who were the fabulous witnesses to my childhood, masters of sneaky tricks, open hearts, and common sense. When I was with them I had no need of the company of other children.

From my secure position I suddenly became aware of the loneliness of the guest, of the longing glances she was casting toward the bottle of juice that stood at the far end of the table next to the green armchair. Then I noticed how she tugged her gaze from the bottle over to the strangers who perhaps at that very moment were deciding her fate, as if searching for an ally among evil connivers, trying to understand what they were whispering about, all huddled together. Her eyes lingered for a moment on my mother's face and wandered to the fingers of her hand, which were busily inserting raisins into my mouth. The sight seemed to fascinate her because she leaned slightly forward, avidly following the industrious movements of my jaw. And then, for the first time, her eyes met mine, and I hastily swallowed the mash of raisins in my mouth, with a clear apprehension of the distress I saw there.

With the innocent heart of a nine-year-old for whom justice is still the most natural path, I stood up, chose a dish of pink and white candy-coated almonds from the table, and approached her.

From close up, I now saw, her eyes were of normal size and naturally elongated, and their thick lashes fluttered when she blinked.

"You have really pretty eyes," I said. "You don't see them because of your glasses."

She didn't move a muscle, just held my gaze as if trying to discern whether I had come over to spy on her, child-shaped bait on a mission from the adults.

"They're tasty." I recommended the candied almonds. "Do you like these? I'm crazy about them."

All at once her face softened. She gazed at me like someone who sees something that has been revealed to her alone, and for the first time since she had entered the room she smiled and her forehead smoothed out.

"Yes, I like them, thank you." The melody of her voice, rich and brave, was a surprise, removed as it was from her weak leg and bad eyes.

I held out the bowl to her. She examined its contents without stirring and then chose two pink ellipses, rolling them in the palm of her hand as if suspicious of them.

"What's your name?"

"Micha."

"I'm Adella."

It seemed she had approved the almonds, because she put one in her mouth and the other one she placed in my hand, motioning that I should put it in my mouth, and then she closed her eyes.

The sounds of an argument arose from the adults' table, but we two were engrossed in the sweetness dissolving on our tongues, giving way to the flavor flooding our taste buds, perhaps sensing in some mysterious way the fatefulness of that instant which would remain seared in both our hearts as the moment marking the birth of the alliance that would bind us from then on. Only when the last trace of the sugar had vanished did we open our eyes and grin at each other.

"I'm going to be a writer when I grow up." I didn't know what made me trust her with my deepest secret.

"That's great," she smiled. "It's good to aim high. Try to remember the taste; maybe one day you'll want to write about it."

"Sure." I moved the bottle of juice closer to her along with a cup and returned to the shelter of my mother, ignoring the questioning look in my Aunt Vika's eyes.

At that moment Yosef decided that it was time for the guest to leave, and he ordered his brother Menashe to take her back to the boarding school. Menashe went out to bring the car, and Lily, who knew the way, was sent to tell Adella to get up. Silence fell around the table as the adults turned toward the girl. Most of them had already forgotten that she was there, and now that her presence was recalled they craned their necks to watch the way she raised herself out of the chair, narrowing their eyes to observe her limp as she traversed the distance to the door. And she, conscious of the examination she was compelled to submit to, didn't deign to so much as glance at them, grasping with both hands the sweater that had been lying in her lap and looking only at the intended groom, as if presenting herself to him as she walked past, doing her best to minimize her limp on her way out. In the vestibule, in full view of the family, she shook out the sweater and shimmied into its sleeves, slowly twisting her torso, balancing on the toes of her good leg to remove her coat from the hook where it was hanging, fumbled for the coat sleeves, couldn't locate the openings and finally shrugged the coat onto her shoulders and disappeared from sight, with Lily hurrying after her to Menashe's car.

"You're all acting like she's a snake about to strike," said the Jerusalem brother who was standing by the door after giving a perfunctory kiss to each of his siblings as he helped his wife into her coat.

"She left without saying goodbye." Vika took pains to criticize her.

"We didn't say goodbye, either," my mother responded, echoing Vika's tone.

"She kissed the *mezuzah*," noted the Jerusalemite, in her favor, as he stood back so his wife could go on ahead.

"She'd better!" Vika had the last word as the door closed behind him.

"Go and play with your cousins already." As if he had only then noticed my presence, Uncle Yosef vented his spleen on me and thus expressed his irritation with my mother. "Go and sit with them: why are you glued to the adults?"

And from that point on what they said, what they proposed, what they planned, who was against Adella and who was for her—it all took place without me.

That same evening I heard my mother talking on the phone to my father, who had been gone for eight months by then, because of his business in Los Angeles.

"They inspected her like a goat in the market," she fumed, "looked her over, weighed and measured her, then sent her home with a kick in the butt." When he appeared to side with his brothers-in-law, she responded shrilly, "She's only eighteen years old, what does she know?"

It seemed that his reply only served to incense her further, and she asked in a hoarse voice, reserved for that question alone: "And where were you all evening yesterday?"

And then immediately backed down and said, "Never mind, it's not important."

At that moment I could tell from the crumpled expression on her face, like that of a little girl who at any moment might burst into tears, that she was feeling lost and helpless, and so I went over to her and hugged her, and she put a loving hand on my head, and it was as if her voice gained strength from my nearness and she recovered her usual tone as she said into the receiver, "If it wasn't for your little boy, who saved the family honor, we would have come out of it like a bunch of villains."

And thus the lines were drawn for the family front concerning Adella. On one side the men—except for Uncle Mordechai, the teacher in Jerusalem—and among them apparently also my father, and with them Vika the big sister, with Aunt Lily unwittingly dragged along behind her, the very Lily who from the moment when she first heard about the orphan who was from our Iranian community had the bright idea to marry her to Uncle Moshe. But when the candidate arrived at my grandfather's house, soaking wet from the pouring rain, she led her over to the armchair and abandoned the girl there, to the prying eyes of the siblings, and only at the end of the evening did Lily return to collect her as though she had deposited an inanimate object on that chair.

And on the other side, two women and a boy. Kindhearted Aunt Esther, whose opinion carried no weight ever since she had been widowed and her only son had left to attend university in Paris and married a non-Jewish Frenchwoman, and with her my mother, whose position was clear and whose rebellious spirit infused me with courage, so that I had stood up and done what I did.

And between the two camps, my Uncle Moshe—concealing his trembling hands underneath tables, gazing at the world like an infant, from childhood always at the mercy of his brothers and sisters, and who, ever since my grandmother died, had been living alone with my grandfather, helping his brothers in their stores in the mornings and in the evenings listening to the stories of his elderly father, brokenhearted by the loss of his wife who had been at his side from the day she turned fourteen.

I tingled with an unfamiliar excitement as I waited impatiently for an entire week until the next meeting with Adella, and I counted down the days until Shabbat would come. If they sat her in the armchair again and placed the bottle of juice at the far edge of the table, I swore, puffing up like a knight in shining armor, that I wouldn't wait until the end of the evening, but would approach her immediately, move the bottle closer to her, bring over a glass and several dishes of refreshments and leave them next to her, then go into the kitchen and pile her plate with the food arranged there on the large brass platters, skipping the dish made with the turkey necks, and every so often I would go to her to ask if she needed anything.

By the time the yearned-for evening finally arrived, the rain had stopped, and my mother and I went to my grandfather's house on foot. She didn't know the answer to my query about whether or not Adella would be there again, just as she had no answer to the question about when my father would be coming back from Los Angeles. Those two question marks continued to float in the air above our heads for the rest of our walk.

The moment I walked in, it was as if the signal had been given to commence the ceremonial sequence that was repeated every Saturday evening, fixed and precise as a law of nature. My mother approaches my grandfather and kisses his hand, and he inverts that same hand and caresses my face with his palm. Now I kiss my grandfather's hand, and he pulls me toward him so that I can also plant a kiss on each of his cheeks. Then he places his hand on my head like a skullcap made flesh and mumbles a blessing. While he is reciting the blessing I stand still as a statue, but my eyes swivel toward the front door to see which of my cousins has arrived.

The instant my grandfather lifts his hand from my head I'm off like a shot, running to my cousins, and we slap and clap hands, hook our feet around each other's ankles to see who can be toppled over first, the entire ritual an expression of our joy at being reunited. When everyone has come inside and the women have placed the baked goods and the pots of food they have prepared on the kitchen counters, the relatives settle themselves around the table and wait for someone to get up and start serving the refreshments, and by then my cousins have all piled into Uncle Moshe's room, and I have assumed my position next to my mother, with the adults.

From the conversation at the table I glean the events of the previous Saturday evening. All the way back to the boarding school in Givat Ada, Menashe and Lily did not exchange one word with Adella, and only after they had dropped her off at the gate and watched her run through the rain toward the building did Lily confess to her brother that she had been mistaken about Adella and she was sorry that she had troubled the family and especially him on this winter's evening by recommending an unsuitable young woman. It was true that she was one of us, which was her most important virtue, but now she suddenly recalled that her daughter Rina had also mentioned that Adella was quite stubborn and sometimes arguments broke out between her and the two girls with whom she shared her room.

On the spot Yosef made the unilateral decision that this girl, damaged both within and without, should be struck from the list, and no one opened his mouth to mention that other than Adella there weren't any candidates on the list. At this point all eyes turned toward Moshe. Over the previous week he had asked several times whether anyone had spoken to Adella and whether she would be willing to come again. Now that he understood that his brother had made the decision for both of them, he was compelled to acquiesce to it with bowed head, as though he had transgressed. To strike her from the list—Yosef repeated his decree above the hunched shape of the intended groom—and to find Moshe a suitable bride.

A whole month passed, and on the Tu Bishvat holiday, the springtime celebration of the New Year of the Trees, Vika brought an assortment of fruits to her father's house, and her sister Lily toasted grains of wheat and transformed them into a tasty treat. The family meetings took place as usual, except that Uncle Moshe's spirits sagged.

Three months had passed since Adella's visit. The Purim holiday was around the corner and the little girls were preparing to dress up as Queen Vashti or Queen Esther. Everyone was waiting to listen to the Scroll of Esther read aloud and to yell and shake their rattles and shout in an explosion of noise every time the name of the villain Haman was uttered, when the air would vibrate with whistles and shrieks and the stamping of feet. This would be followed by the reading out of the list of names of Haman's sons, as the clamor increased in an earsplitting cacophony.

And still no applicant was located among the extended family for the position of wife for Uncle Moshe, not among those who attended our synagogue and not among the customers at my uncles' stores, who were also Iranian. Despite all their efforts, no appropriate bride was found for their silent, single brother, about whom, other than his kind heart and his beautiful head of hair, which was already threaded with glints of grey, they were hard-pressed to find anything praiseworthy to add.

At one of the Saturday-evening gatherings, Lily suddenly mentioned that she had news about Adella.

My gaze flashed toward Uncle Moshe, and I saw how he abruptly lifted his head and blinked rapidly.

"What news?" asked Yosef, and although his voice plainly conveyed his antipathy toward Adella, it was also clear that Lily was permitted to continue.

The hesitation in Lily's voice as she recounted her visit to the boarding school during the Purim festival gave way to enthusiasm as she described how her heart had leapt at the sight of the traditional Haman's Ears triangular pastries that Adella had baked, which were displayed on a platter in the Teachers' Room, beautiful and symmetrical as if a machine and not a human hand had turned them out. In a kind of revelation—and at this point Lily touched her hand to her heart—she declared that she had recognized then with every fiber of her being that whoever had prepared those hamantaschen was the right wife for Moshe and the right woman for a family that owned a bakery, and that she should have followed her initial instinct and understood that the stubbornness which the young woman had cultivated was no more than a protective shell in the environment where she had grown up and should thus be counted as a virtue and not a vice. Moreover, Rina herself had confessed that once she looked into the disagreements with the roommates, it emerged that most of the time Adella had been in the right. Lily related how she had remained at the boarding school until she managed to locate Adella in her room and ask her to come out.

"Weren't you embarrassed to go to her room?" Vika shot at her.

Moshe's eyes were riveted on Lily in supplication.

"Adella came to the doorway," Lily continued, and stood there without inviting Lily to come in. At that moment, taken aback by Adella's reaction, Lily found herself at a loss for words and finally she stammered that they hadn't had a chance to talk since that Saturday-evening visit.

Adella didn't answer right away; most likely she was recalling that Saturday-evening visit, and finally she asked what they had to talk about.

Lily replied immediately that she was curious to hear what Adella's impressions were of her family, of her brother Moshe. And to this Adella responded that she had no opinion about him. They hadn't allowed her to exchange half a word with him. And with that she went back into her room and closed the door.

"*Chutzpah!* What nerve!" Aunt Vika spat, looking around and nodding, anticipating the others' support.

Uncle Moshe continued to look fixedly at Aunt Lily's mouth, refusing to accept that this was the end of the story.

"Next Shabbat there will be another woman here!" Vika announced.

A surprised hush descended on the room. Before Lily had brought up Adella's name, Vika hadn't mentioned anything about a possible bride.

"Who?" Moshe dared to ask.

"You'll see. She's pretty," she promised.

The candidate was a new customer at the bakery who

bought challah bread every Friday, a thirty-year-old, religiously observant woman who had been divorced for eight years and described herself as the owner of a small business. Despite the aversion to her divorced status and the speculation over the flaw that had prevented her from finding a husband for eight long years, the woman was invited to the regular Saturday-evening gathering. To everyone's mortification, she fled before her backside could make contact with a chair. Straight after she entered the house and slipped off her coat in one graceful movement, hanging it in the appointed place with the appropriate ceremony, the woman approached the potential groom whom she had glimpsed several times at the bakery. She introduced herself and held out her hand. Moshe stared at the extended fingers, and his reaction was slow to come. The rest of the family held its collective breath as he finally brought out his own hand to shake hers, but the woman was so shocked at the sight of that trembling appendage that she did not tarry until the two hands might meet. Turning on her heel, she grabbed her coat off the rack and marched out the door. Moshe's head dropped heavily to his chest, and Vika cursed the short-lived candidate, entreating the Lord never to bless her with sons.

At the end of that evening, overwhelmingly tarnished by the humiliation with which it was set in motion, Esther wondered aloud why, in fact, the orphan from the boarding school had been disqualified. Moshe's eyes gleamed, and he watched his sister in surprise, brimming with anticipation. The answer, which everyone other than the innocent Esther knew full well, was that back then they had still believed that they would easily find a more suitable match. And then Lily repeated her tale of the rows of perfect Purim pastries and her conversation with Adella, except that this time Yosef didn't allow her to finish her story about the encounter.

"There are other women in the world," he said, cutting her

off, and I looked into Uncle Moshe's eyes and watched as the brief spark of light that had shone in them faded away.

During the following month my aunts were busy setting out vats of boiling water in their yards in which they would immerse their dishes to make them kosher for Pesach, scrubbing every inch of their homes and checking with tweezers by candlelight to ensure that no leavened crumbs were still to be found, preparing all the traditional foods for the evening of the Pesach Seder, crushing almonds, dates, walnuts, and spices and steeping them in wine. Over the course of that month two more prospective brides arrived with their families, gave the groom a once-over, took their leave politely, and refrained from a second visit. And three weeks later a pleasant woman showed up, who had received Vika's seal of approval and kindled hope among the brothers, until it came to light that she had two young children whose existence was revealed only by chance, and it was suspected that she was motivated by the desire for a roof over their heads and wouldn't have much time to spare for Moshe.

Moshe attended synagogue with the men, but his mouth did not open to recite with them the blessing "Wishing you many years of life," and Lily did not respond joyfully with the women, "May you be blessed with a hundred such good years."

Ever since her change of heart, one of her eyes still swollen and bloodshot after her son accidentally poked her with a stalk of spring onion at the Seder table, Lily provided the family at the weekly gatherings with continuous updates about Adella: in two months, at the end of the school year, she planned to leave the boarding school and move to a one-room apartment in Or Akiva, where the first six months' rent would be paid by the Ministry of Social Services, giving her time to stand on her own feet. She didn't mention the man with the overfull mouth of teeth who still appeared sometimes at the gate, or how Adella ignored him and his insistent pleading in contravention of her aunts' wishes. The boarding school offered her a part-time job at minimum wage, and she was keeping that in mind as a last resort, while meanwhile, following up on an ad she had seen by chance in a local paper, she had found a position, at a miniscule salary, at a lawyers' office in the city of Hadera. Every Friday, on her day off, she promised to visit Mrs. Berta the Holocaust survivor and then to come to the boarding school, to embrace the teachers and make cookies in the kitchen, and to meet with the younger girls, because by then all the girls her own age would have left.

Six months had passed since the inauguration of the campaign to find Moshe a bride, six months during which we marked the period between Pesach and Shavuot by counting down the fifty days and symbolically renewing our spirit, and then Shavuot arrived, a holiday I especially liked because of the flowers, and the sweet date pudding that my mother always prepared. During those six months—I learned this many years later—Adella successfully evaded the man who waited patiently at the boarding-school gate. And also during this period, my grandfather's health declined, and he often fell down at home. Now he needed constant supervision, and so it became more urgent to find a wife for Moshe.

With no alternative, through gritted teeth, Lily was instructed to try to make things right with Adella, but it was already September. The next time she went to bring food to Rina, planning to stop by the office to ask for Adella's address in Or Akiva, to Lily's surprise she found Adella in the kitchen, preparing special apple tarts for the girls for the New Year and Shabbat. The following day, downcast and in a low voice, Lily told her siblings that Adella was prepared to return for another visit, but she had insisted on two conditions.

Tension filled the air. Moshe gazed pleadingly at his brothers.

"We didn't even say we want her, and she's making demands already?" Vika seethed with contempt.

"What are the conditions?" the muscles moved in Moshe's jaw.

Lily blurted out Adella's terms, the words tumbling over each other in her haste to be done with the telling: to speak in private with her intended, and to speak in private with the family representative.

"In private and in private!" Yosef mimicked her.

"Never!" Vika was on her feet. "Our family is beneath her? She can limp her way over to another family. She won't find a better one than ours."

"She isn't only getting the family, she's getting Abba and Moshe." My mother reminded everyone of what they had preferred to overlook. "And much as we love them, we have to be reasonable." Here she turned to Moshe. "Do you want to meet her, Moshe?" and Moshe, although he wasn't used to being addressed directly with a question, answered immediately, "Yes."

"You'll meet her, don't worry." Vika soothed him with prophetic words: "In the end she'll come crawling with no conditions, and she'll thank us, too."

The New Year was drawing nearer, and Moshe, who was confined to the house to take care of my grandfather, was needed in the stores more than ever. He only managed to get to them to help out his brothers when one of the sisters dragged herself away from her housework to sit with her father.

Moshe and his father sat like mourners at the holiday table, each immersed in his own worries, and for the entirety of Yom Kippur Moshe fasted and prayed with great conviction.

Once again, Lily was sent to talk to Adella. On Saturday evening, when Shabbat was over, she appeared looking extremely pale and delivered the news that in addition to the two previous conditions—to speak in private with Moshe and to speak in private with the representative of the family—a new condition had been added. Before anything else, there would be a private conversation with the groom's family physician.

A heavy silence descended when Lily had concluded her mumbled message. No one said mockingly, "in private, in private," and other than on Moshe's face and mine, there were no furtive smiles. It was clear to everyone that surrender was the only option, and their blood boiled with the realization that a limping, half-blind young girl had brought the proud family to its knees. But that anger was tinged with a foreboding of sweet revenge, and the knowledge, I sensed with certainty, that it would be exacted once the intended bride had joined the family—then they would show her, and she would finally understand what her place was and never again dare to wound their pride and humiliate them.

Yosef threw back his shoulders and, struggling to conceal his vexation, he boomed, "Let her come! Her conditions don't scare us!"

"I saw you smile," my mother said when we were back at home. "What are you so happy about?"

"I'm happy for Uncle Moshe."

"That's nice." She didn't see any reason to argue.

I had trouble falling asleep that night. I hadn't lied to my mother about being happy for my uncle, but what I really felt was a sense of the victory of justice in the struggle between the young girl and the adults who didn't want her, and I suddenly remembered the picture of David and Goliath that hung on the wall in my cousin Yair's bedroom.

The visit with the doctor, my mother reported to my father on the phone, took place on a Friday morning, and Adella went alone. Several days before the appointment, my mother drove her brother Moshe to the clinic so he could sign a waiver of confidentiality. On the Friday morning, Vika tried her best to go with her, but Adella insisted that she be unaccompanied when she spoke to the doctor. What Adella asked the doctor and what his responses were, no one knew. Yosef, who visited the doctor to see what he could find out about the meeting, pretending that he just happened to be passing by, was curtly informed that the contents of the meeting were strictly confidential, and was also told by the doctor that he should go to the synagogue and say a prayer of gratitude for his brother Moshe's good fortune.

The meeting with the groom-to-be was supposed to have taken place on the following Friday morning, but it was postponed owing to disagreements about the location. At first, Aunt Vika, who was mediating the issue, was adamant that it should take place at her father's home, where Moshe lived, and in that way solve the problem of who would be looking after the old man on the day. Adella demanded that Moshe come to her room in Or Akiva. After a period of negotiation, Adella agreed that the meeting could be held at my mother's house. Vika persisted in her stipulation that she be present during the meeting, insisting on some measure of control over the proceedings, but Adella dismissed the possibility out of hand and finally conceded that if someone had to be present, it would be "Micha, the boy who offered me almonds on my first visit."

Vika, anxious that I was too young to be able to understand the essence of the conversation and to subsequently provide an accurate report, suggested one of the older girl cousins instead. But Adella wouldn't budge, and the haggling reached a deadlock.

My mother, secretly proud that of all the houses Adella had chosen hers, and of all the children had chosen me, made me party to her deliberations about which room she should prepare for the important meeting between Adella and Moshe.

We agreed that the most pleasant room in the house was not the room of Rafi, my older brother, but the room that belonged to my sister Yarden, who had just begun her army service. This was mainly because of the east-facing window and the beautiful light that spilled through it. Together we cleaned the room. My mother placed a brush in my hands and demonstrated how to scrub the shutters, and when I was done she inspected and approved my work. Next we washed the windows and the floor. After that she instructed me to bring in two comfortable chairs from the kitchen, which we arranged facing each other, separated by a small table on which we placed a single rose in a vase, a straw basket of sweet-smelling pine cones, a bottle of cola, two glasses and cookies which my mother had baked specially to break the Yom Kippur fast and saved in the freezer. Finally, my mother had me switch on the nightlight at the head of the bed, and we stood and admired the soft glow that illuminated the distant corner.

"You'll sit here," my mother directed, pointing at the chair near Yarden's desk, where pictures of brightly colored birds adorned the facing wall. "And you sit with your back to them. Give them privacy, so they won't even know you're in the room."

I was overwhelmed by a sense of the momentous nature of the event. I was the boy who had been chosen to witness the secret meeting. A new story was about to be added to my growing treasure trove of tales, one that I might use when I grew up and became a writer.

Moshe, pale and excited, was the first to arrive. My mother finger-combed his hair as she led him to the designated room. She showed him how to interlace his fingers to keep them from trembling and how to wedge his hands between his knees, out of sight of the woman who would be sitting opposite him. "And smile a lot. You have beautiful teeth. Show her," she counselled him.

Adella was dropped at our house, a few minutes late, by my Aunt Lily and my Uncle Menashe. On the doorstep Menashe said that he had left his store during the busiest hours on Friday morning, and while still in mid-sentence he turned and walked out. Lily hurried to keep up with him.

Adella tarried at the entrance. She scanned the room until her eyes met mine and her features relaxed. Only then did she step inside and shut the door behind her. My mother came out and said with festive gaiety, "Welcome to my home. Moshe is already waiting for you," and Adella thanked her and followed her to Yarden's room. My mother stood back to allow me to walk in, gave me a little push and closed the door.

I sat in my chair and instantly disobeyed my mother. I didn't turn away, but leaned back in my seat the better to observe them.

Adella sat down opposite Uncle Moshe and placed her purse on the floor by her feet. He followed every move she made, gazing at her, and they sat there like that, looking at each other. She smiled first, blossoming before him radiantly, and he responded with a wide smile of his own, perhaps recalling my mother's advice. Almost a year had gone by since their previous meeting, a long period of time during which the start of winter gave way to the end of summer and the gloomy fall, and sweaters to cotton shirts and then back to sweaters again. A chunk of time during which—and this she couldn't know—a series of prospective wives had come and gone, and yet here they were facing one another as if the hand of fate itself had intervened. The thought that this meeting in my sister's sun-filled room was somehow ordained from on high filled me with joy as I sat there, never taking my eyes off them, but trying to minimize my presence and sit perfectly still.

"At least today you didn't get soaked." Moshe finally spoke.

Her face fell slightly. Perhaps she was recalling the way she had been received by his siblings on that rainy Saturday evening.

"It's autumn now, and somehow you've managed to get sunburnt," my uncle added quickly, smiling, and I wondered if he had noticed how her color had heightened and was trying to distract her with a joke. Did my uncle possess that level of sensitivity? The ability to respond so quickly? But here I had heard with my own ears the playfulness in his tone, as if right before my eyes he was hatching out of his shell and becoming someone else.

"The sun had its plans, but it didn't get that far." Her features softened, and he noticed and smiled.

"You met with Dr. Aharonov?" He confronted her with the blunt question.

"Yes."

"And did he tell you what you wanted to hear?"

"I needed to understand the situation precisely." She offered an apologetic sentence without apologizing.

"You thought it was Parkinson's?"

"He said it isn't."

"It isn't."

"That's what he said. Nice man, Dr. Aharonov."

"He's saved me more than once."

"Yes, he told me."

There was a brief silence, as though the first mine had been defused and now they could cautiously proceed.

And that's how their conversation began, with short sentences and simple words. Where the sentences conducted one dialogue and the expressions in their eyes conducted another, meandering, casting about for clues, seeking confirmation, granting confirmation. She asked many questions, spoke a lot; he responded in brief, and mostly listened to her. Gradually her sentences became longer, but she continued to use language that was direct and unadorned. It appeared that my presence was forgotten because she spoke to him as though they were alone. One day I would tell myself that it was my first lesson in collecting material before sitting down to write. I could see but was not seen in an encounter between two people who were groping their way toward each other. They spoke of the schools they had attended and the friends, most of whom had betrayed them, and the things they liked to do, and the many things they wanted but had not yet achieved, and about the painful longings of people whose eyes see clearly but whose hands find it difficult to reach out and grasp.

She told him about the boarding school where she had lived from age ten, and described her old room in detail—there were three beds in the room and beside each bed a small cupboard that could be locked. That cupboard contained all her possessions and her clothes, and also, from ninth grade, a book about the Warsaw Ghetto given to her by Mrs. Berta, whom she had visited once a week for two years as part of a volunteer project at the boarding school, and who had taught her a lot. Adella had continued to visit her even after the project was over, and after she had left the school. She still visited her sometimes, and she spoke to her on the phone every Friday and wished her a good Shabbat. She had occasionally spent weekends with her, but usually stayed at the nearly empty boarding school with two other girls. Her roommates had invited her to come home with them, and once she agreed to go with one of them and had met her large and noisy family, and then returned to the school feeling sad. From then on she preferred to remain at the quiet school. He told her, in the scant sentences he uttered, about his only friend from his school days who had left the country many years before, about his love for his mother who had never once complained, about the herbs he cultivated in pots, about his dream to work in a spice shop.

Decades later I would retrieve the memory of the sounds and colors of that scene, of the shimmering room, as though the sun had channeled all its brilliance through Yarden's window, of Adella's amber eyes shining in the light, of the glimmers of silver sparkling in Uncle Moshe's hair, of Adella's clear voice, Uncle Moshe's hesitant one, the sound of his sudden sighs, and the silence between their sentences. I wasn't yet ten years old, and still I was acutely aware of the energy quivering in the air between the two people in the room, conscious that I was witnessing an extraordinary moment.

Suddenly Moshe glanced at the clock, and as if rousing himself from a dream he said in a panic, "I have to get back to my brother's store."

"And I also have to get back to Or Akiva." She too rose to her feet. "But we'll have lots more time to talk."

It seemed that her response hadn't reached him as he burst out of the room, as if he hadn't been sitting there comfortably for all that time. And unfazed by his strange behavior she just retrieved her purse and looked over at me.

"How are you, Micha?"

"Fine."

"Is it true, what your uncle told me?"

"It must be. Uncle Moshe never lies."

"That's good," she said.

"And what you said, was it true?"

"I lie sometimes, but what I said was true."

At that moment my mother walked into the room and, not wasting a moment on small talk, she asked, "Was it all right?"

"It was just fine," Adella responded pleasantly. "And the cookies were delicious."

"Cookies baked for Yom Kippur have to be tasty."

My mother followed her to the front door, expecting more, but Adella just turned and said, "I know where to catch the bus to the Central Bus Station. Thank you very much, and you too, Micha," and she was gone, leaving my mother hungry for information. Since her curiosity hadn't been satisfied, she tried to pump me for details. But my loyalty already lay with Adella, and so I said, "You told me not to listen, so I didn't. I looked at the encyclopedia."

The news that the meeting had gone well spread like wildfire among the siblings. But it was still too early to seal the deal, for there remained one more obstacle to overcome. Adella had yet to come face-to-face with the family representative. With no need for discussion it was clear to all that Yosef, the eldest, only seventeen years his father's junior, was the only choice. Once again the family attempted to hold the meeting at my grandfather's house, which was also Moshe's house, and once again she demurred. Adella also firmly rejected the proposal that they meet at Yosef's house on another Friday for the Shabbat meal and that she sleep over at the home of one of the sisters.

My mother, buoyed by the success of the meeting that had taken place at her house, proud of the fact that something in the atmosphere of the home which she had cultivated—and perhaps also her idea to set out the pinecones which had occurred to her at the last moment—had contributed to the flowering of feelings, suggested that they meet in her living room, while she herself would wait in the kitchen and block her ears.

Other than the three of them—she promised—not a soul would be present. Yosef, who was accustomed to his wishes being complied with unquestioningly, was compelled this once to bargain and had no choice but to compromise. He struggled to conceal his fury at being forced to give in to his sister's idea, and so as to retain some vestige of his pride, insisted that he be the one to choose the day and time. Finally, a meeting was set for Adella and my Uncle Yosef.

Adella arrived early on the appointed date, and I opened the door to her on my way out.

"My mother told me that you said I should leave the house." I rebuked her as I turned back to switch off the television news, which was marking a month since the plane carrying Israeli navigator Ron Arad had crashed in southern Lebanon, where he had been taken prisoner by the Amal Shi'ite terrorist group.

"Yes. Because it won't be nice like the meeting with your other uncle," she said.

My mother burst out of the kitchen, a joyful expression on her face, as though she wanted to signal to Adella that she already considered her a part of the family, and to encourage her to stand firm in the confrontation with her inflexible and tyrannical elder brother.

But Adella didn't return her welcoming expression. She peered anxiously into the house and asked whether she had arrived first. When this was confirmed, almost apologetically she asked if she could check.

"Check what?" asked my mother, but she seemed to be talking to thin air, because Adella was already out of earshot.

Adella walked past the dining-room table where refreshments had been aesthetically arranged and investigated each of the three rooms, including the bedroom with the ensuite bathroom and the separate bathroom between the two children's rooms. She returned to the living room and peeked behind the furniture and the curtains.

Clearly shocked, my mother motioned that I should leave the house, but I lingered at the front door, curious to see what would happen next.

"Everything's fine," Adella confirmed, and she placed her purse on the table. But despite the conciliatory aspect with which Adella regarded my mother, feature by feature the face looking back at her was colored by anger and insult. I observed my mother anxiously. It was an unequivocal expression. I recognized it well. Its meaning was that the die was cast, and there would be no absolution.

"I came a little early," Adella began in a friendly tone, but my mother didn't wait to hear the rest of the sentence. She tossed off a curt, "Go already," in my direction but didn't check to see whether or not I obeyed, and turned on her heel to reenter the kitchen, sparks of rage crackling around her body. Because at that very moment the bell rang, she walked over to open the front door and then immediately turned away and disappeared into the kitchen.

Adella and Uncle Yosef were left facing one another.

"Here I am," he finally said.

"I got here first." She signaled that if it was war he wanted, she was ready for him.

"So sit down first." He pointed at the armchair, and it wasn't clear whether this was another challenge or if an offer of a ceasefire had escaped his throat. "And you, scram," he said to me, and before I slammed the door I managed to glimpse that Adella was walking toward the seat he had indicated while he collapsed his great girth into the armchair opposite.

When I returned two hours later I found my mother alone in the house, still fuming.

"What happened?" I asked.

"They talked."

"Did they make an agreement?"

"The wedding's in two months. And you're going to be the *shushbin*, the one who gives her away; that's what she wants," my mother went into her room and left me alone with the sensational news. For a moment I hesitated, unsure as to whether I should follow and try to mollify her, but I could already hear the sound of the key turning as she locked her door.

I went to my room and found the dictionary: "*shushbin* (literally 'friend' or 'acquaintance'): the one who escorts the groom or the bride to the wedding canopy at a wedding ceremony, usually a relative or close friend."

Here, I knew, was where our paths diverged, my mother's and mine; her incapacity for forgiveness, and my innate tendency to compromise. For the rest of that day until I fell asleep I held fast to the thought—of all the girls at her boarding school, of all the teachers who had taught her, of all the people she knew in the world, of all my girl cousins and boy cousins and all my uncles and aunts—Adella had chosen me to be her bridesman and escort her to her wedding canopy. And since we weren't yet related, that meant that I was her closest friend in the world.

My mother continued to provide my father with telephone updates about the family affairs. Now, I noted, she spoke about Adella with bitterness, finding fault with whatever she did. A month and a half before the wedding—I learned from my mother's conversations with my father—Adella vacated her free lodgings in Or Akiva and rented a room not far from my grandfather's house in the apartment of a nurse who was absent for most of the day since she worked privately with the chronically ill.

Every afternoon Adella would buy groceries and go to my grandfather's house to make dinner. Sometimes one of the siblings would join them and report to the others about what she said and what she prepared. After dinner Adella would wash the dishes and the kitchen floor, join my grandfather and Uncle Moshe who were watching television, and while she sat with them she would fold laundry, reinforce the stitches in their trousers, replace missing buttons. At ten o'clock she would take her leave without so much as a handshake and return to her rented room. In this way—it was mostly the sisters who discerned this—a fondness developed between Adella and Moshe, and they often exchanged smiles. At every visit Moshe would announce the number of days that remained until their wedding.

My mother persevered in her anger toward Adella and refused to meet her and even forbade me to accompany her to my grandfather's house, despite the many times Adella sent her regards. Then she took to visiting her father on weekday mornings and stopped going to his house on Saturday evenings. And yet, I gleaned from the information she provided to my father on the phone, she was clearly ensuring that she was kept abreast of the goings-on at those family get-togethers.

"You hate her so much, just because she snooped around the rooms that day?" I dared to inquire in a moment of closeness.

"I don't hate her, I just don't think about her. First of all because your sister and your brother are coming this week, and second of all because I love your uncle. And I'm worried. She isn't what she wants us to see; she's something else."

My mother's complicated words hit a nerve. Ever since I heard Adella say to my Uncle Yosef in a steady voice, "I got here first," it was as if all at once the pretense of the poor little girl squashed into the green armchair had fallen away, and her true nature had surfaced.

And so I was momentarily alarmed when my mother said one day, "Today after school I have to bring you to her."

"To who? To Adella?"

"Yes."

"But, why?"

"Moshe promised her."

"She asked him?"

"Apparently."

"Why?"

"Because you're her bridesman. Wear the blue shirt."

"So you aren't mad at her anymore?"

"I will never forgive her." Her face still wore the wounded expression she had assumed on that day.

That same expression remained fixed on her visage for the entire journey, until they were standing face to face in the doorway.

"Thank you for coming." Adella opened the door wide and smiled happily, and all my concerns evaporated in the light that beamed from her eyes. Adella was back to being the girl who had sat in Yarden's room opposite Uncle Moshe.

"I'll be back in an hour to get him." No change registered on the frozen face of my mother lit by Adella's radiant smile.

"Please come in. I welcome you with all my heart." Adella regarded my mother fondly above my head.

"One hour to the minute." She turned and descended the stairs.

Adella and I watched my mother's back recede until it disappeared, and then she grabbed my hand, like a child-snatcher in the movies, and pulled me inside.

"Do you like real hot chocolate, Micha?" She leaned toward me conspiratorially, and with her free hand slammed the door shut as she led me to the kitchen, which was redolent with a sweet smell, and sat me down by the little table where three mugs were waiting. Once again I was frightened. Without my mother by my side I was at the mercy of the whims of this strange woman who had kidnapped me. I sat and watched fearfully as she lit the flame under a small saucepan.

"Hot chocolate made from real chocolate. I've already heated it, and it's almost ready. Now we add this . . ." she slid half a bar of chocolate into the small, steaming pot, and smiled at me promisingly.

I barely recognized the girl scrunched into the armchair at my grandfather's house. Neither did I see the young woman, her face full of suspicion, who had made a circuit of the house before the meeting with my Uncle Yosef. Now she cast her arms wide as if embracing the air.

"Do you remember my name?" she gave me a penetrating stare.

"Adella."

"Right. And you're Micha, I also remember. How old are you, Micha?"

"I'm ten."

"Ten is already a big boy," she flattered me. "Do you know why I asked your mother to bring you?"

"Because I'm your bridesman."

"That's right. Did she explain to you what that means?"

"I saw in the dictionary."

"Great. Have they bought you a suit yet?"

"I have a suit from my cousin's bar mitzvah six months ago."

"Great. And a tie?"

"No."

"So you need a tie. I'll bring you one. Here, now let's drink the hot chocolate. Just be careful, it's really hot. And then I'll show you two surprises, and you'll help me choose something for my wedding dress."

"I've never chosen a wedding dress." I was alarmed.

"Neither have I. But first let's drink the hot chocolate."

Adella served me a mug steaming with the powerful pungent smell of chocolate and as though we already shared the tradition, we closed our eyes the moment the thick, hot liquid touched our lips, succumbing to its flow from the tip of the tongue along its length until it reached our throats. The two of us sipped the drink and felt how it spread out inside our bodies, filling us with sweet joy, dissolving all suspicion.

With the taste of chocolate still in our mouths, Adella beckoned that I should follow her to the guestroom and pointed at a sweater spread out on the sofa. I had never seen another sweater like it, decorated with lace and buttons and beads and shiny ribbons tied in bows along its sleeves and around the neckline; a royal article of clothing whose brilliant colors were like the feathers of the parrot in the picture tacked to the wall opposite Yarden's desk.

"What do you think, Micha?"

"Really beautiful." My faith in her was completely restored through the loveliness displayed before me. "It's a sweater from an enchanted kingdom."

"I'm happy that you think so," she said in a gentle voice.

"So many colors. Where did you buy it?"

"I didn't buy it. I made it myself."

"Really? All by yourself?" Now a new personage joined those of the pathetic Adella and the malicious Adella.

"Yes. It's—like you said—a sweater from an enchanted kingdom. Whoever wears it becomes a princess. I have a few like it. Each one is different. I gave one to the director of the boarding school when I left. And now come and look at this." She motioned that I should kneel beside her.

From underneath the desk she pulled out a large suitcase,

positioning it between us. I watched curiously as her fingers flipped open the top like the cover of a gigantic book to reveal old notebooks arranged one on top of the other.

"Where's this from? The boarding school?"

"No. Mrs. Berta gave it to me. I'll tell you her story one day. She's a very important woman in my life."

She pulled out a notebook with a white cover and opened it. A small piece of fabric was sewn to the top half of the page, and beneath it were two handwritten paragraphs, one in English and one in Hebrew.

"This is the Cotton Notebook," she said softly, as if willing to divulge just a sliver of a secret. "Today we'll only look at the first page. I love cotton the most, so we'll start with cotton. Here, now touch this fabric."

I copied her movement, rubbing my thumb back and forth above my index finger, sliding it across the piece of cloth I was holding and looking at Adella questioningly.

"Try to find the heart of the fabric," she answered my inquiring gaze. "Yes, yes, every piece of cloth has a heart. Fabric is a living thing, it breathes and its heart beats, and if you hold it gently but firmly, the way a doctor takes someone's pulse, you can feel its heart."

I crumpled the piece of cotton in my hand and leaned toward it, straining my eyes and my ears in my search for its heart.

"Do you feel it?"

"I don't know . . ."

"You'll learn to find it. I can feel the heart of the fabric even without touching it. You'll learn too. In the end you will also love cotton," she promised. "Have you learned at school about the slaves in America?"

"No."

"They brought slaves to America to grow and pick the cotton. Today they don't have slaves any more, thank God." She carefully placed the notebook at the bottom of the suitcase and said, "One by one I'll teach you about all the types of fabric. Now I want you to see the fabric for the wedding dress, and then we'll continue with the other kinds. Wait here for a minute."

At that moment I was completely bewitched by her, and the fear my mother had instilled in me vanished almost completely. I sat staring at the door, longing for her to return. When she did it was as though a different woman had taken her place, one who was wearing a wedding dress. She stood for a moment, perhaps taking in my look of surprise, giving me time to adjust to this other woman. Then she came up very close to me, "Touch the collar," she coaxed as she arched her neck so that I could reach it. "Just watch out for the pins."

I stretched a tentative hand toward the slim gold collar that was attached to the dress with sewing pins.

"Now the essence of the fabric is seeping into your fingers and it will stay there for a long time. I'll change out of the dress and tell you about this fabric."

I couldn't feel a thing in the fingers that had touched the collar and yet I still held them at a distance from my body. Poison: the certain knowledge floated up within me—she had put poison on the collar.

When she reappeared, dressed in her regular clothes, she looked like Adella again and she launched into an explanation about the golden silk collar, fashioned of a wild silk known as Muga, withdrew a blue notebook from the suitcase, and said, "I'll show you one wool and one silk. This is the Wool Notebook. And the first one is the best and most expensive wool, cashmere." She breathed the name in a whisper, held it out to me so I could touch it and watched my fingers.

"Cashmere is a kind of goat. It's also the name of a country near India. Do you know how many goats it takes to have enough wool for one sweater?"

"How many?"

"Three. And it keeps you eight times warmer than regular sheep's wool does and weighs one-third, which is why it's
so light and downy. Whoever wears cashmere feels as though
someone is caressing them. It's the finest fiber in the world. Do
you know what fiber is?"

By the end of the visit I had given myself over wholly to
stories about fabric. We spent a long time kneeling in front
of the open suitcase as if at an altar. And I, I had no idea that
I was receiving an important lesson in the sensations born of
touch, how they flowed from the heart and scattered like fire-
works through the cells of the body. I extended my hands and
ran the cloth through my fingers like someone learning a new
language who could already identify the sounds of some of
the words.

In the silent moment when I was immersed in the texture
of the silk, the doorbell jangled and pulled us rudely out of
the bubble that had formed around us. Adella was the first to
regain her composure, tugging the notebook from my fingers,
placing it in the belly of the suitcase, swiftly clicking the lid and
pushing the case back under the desk.

"That must be your mother. We'll continue next time."

The open door revealed my mother's still-furious expression, except that now there was the added flashing of her eyes
between the two faces before her, as she searched for a sign of
something certain, if concealed.

"Maybe now you'll come in—"

"Get your coat." She waved me over and turned to the stairs.
Behind her back I took my leave of Adella with a surreptitious
wave, and when she reciprocated with a furtive gesture which
mimicked mine, our pact of confidentiality was sealed.

We walked to the street, my hand in hers, and didn't exchange a word. Suddenly my mother turned to me, her eyes
scouring my face. "What did you do there?"

"Nothing."

"What do you mean nothing? She must have given you something to eat."

"She made me hot chocolate."

"That's all?"

"Yes."

"And what did you do?"

"We looked at her wedding dress."

"Is it nice?"

"Yes. It's not finished yet. She asked me if the collar suits her. It's made of golden silk."

My mother stopped short in the middle of the sidewalk. "She tried on the dress for you?"

"Yes."

"Who else was with you in the house?"

"No one."

"There must have been someone else there, no? She works at the hospital or something like that?"

"I don't know."

"The owner of the apartment."

"She wasn't there."

"She tried the dress on in front of you?"

"Yes."

"She took off her clothes in front of you?"

"No. She went into the next room."

My mother's eyes searched my face. "I could tell you were lying to me. The minute the door opened I could tell that something wasn't right."

"What's not right? Everything was fine until you got there."

"I shouldn't have left you there." She started walking again, dragging me along behind her.

"You could have stayed. She invited you."

"Very nice of her. And for your information that was the last time. The visits are over. The next time you see her and her dress will be at the wedding—and that's it. And after the wedding there won't be any more visits."

My hand crushed inside my mother's, I tried to match her strides, as her anger propelled her forward with increasing speed, and my eyes welled with tears.

I could still hear the sound of the gentle rustling and feel the pleasurable sensation of the Muga silk, which according to Adella's handwritten entry in the notebook is considered the most precious silk in the world, golden in color, with a lifespan of fifty years, produced only in the Brahmaputra Valley, from the fibers of the cocoon of the Muga silkworm larva. The length of each fiber is one kilometer or 3,281 feet and it weighs ninety grams or about three ounces and maybe at this very minute—I smiled to myself as I raced along beside my mother and felt my fingertips tingling with the memory of the texture—maybe at this exact moment Adella was bending over the table and sewing the collar of her wedding dress with the tiny bit of leftover silk which she found by chance in the bargain bin at the fabric store, a little golden scrap born in the Brahmaputra Valley which a month from now would adorn the throat of a bride at a wedding hall in Ramat Gan.

They didn't bother with the henna ceremony. That pre-wedding ritual had all the things I loved—unbridled joy, ululations, loud music and dancing, tarboosh hats, white and gold caftans, brightly colored garments handed down from generation to generation, candles and flowers, presents for the bride and the groom.

They didn't have any of it. And the wedding ceremony, usually held at the home of the bride at dusk when the community rabbi delivers the Seven Blessings, which are the heart of the event, was combined with the rest of the ceremony, and almost all the people who were chosen to recite them were there, even the couple from Jerusalem with all their children.

And so the "Diamonds" wedding hall was brimming with people, lots of children, men and boys in suits, and heavily made-up women. The sounds of the band merged with the greetings, and a young actress hired to organize the dancing led a chain of children holding hands from the dance floor to the decorated tables and around the dais with the wedding canopy, its sides upholstered with artificial flowers.

My mother arrived surrounded by her three children: me, my sister Yarden, who was already nearing the end of her army service, and my brother Rafi, who had finished his mandatory service and had decided to sign on for an additional year.

Hope had flared briefly that my father might arrive in honor of the occasion, but he explained in one of their phone calls that he hadn't found the time to obtain some document or other that was necessary for him to make the trip, which was an indication to me of the inferior status of this wedding. Maybe his absence was the reason why my aunts and uncles deluged me with love and I was showered with hugs even from relatives I rarely saw, some of whom I didn't recognize. As usual, my cousins and I greeted one another with the familiar punches, jabs, and attempts to trip up each other as we raced among the guests.

My mother, a bundle of nerves, ordered me to sit still and trapped me in a chair wedged between hers and my brother's. At a certain point she turned away from me to tell a woman I didn't know about the Shabbat when my Uncle Moshe was called to read from the Torah at the synagogue, and how the sprays of cologne had rained down on him from the women's section as if gushing from a faucet, and the woman reciprocated with a story about the time her son read from the Torah, and a conversation ensued between them. I chose that moment and the surrounding commotion to slip into the crowd in search of Adella, who I hadn't seen since the day when she showed me her wedding gown.

In a corner of the hall, hidden behind a fabric partition, I found the groom with my Uncle Yosef and my Aunt Lily, grasping his painful right leg. Lily swore that she had walked into every store until she found the most delicate glass of all and reassured him that with all the experience he had accumulated stamping on a dozen glasses he had no reason to worry. But it was plain to see that her words only caused his hands to tremble more violently.

I wandered behind the dais where the wedding canopy was set up and then over to the kitchen and discovered Adella in a small room near the entrance. If it hadn't been for the wedding dress, which I remembered, the one with the gold collar, it's unlikely that I would have recognized her. A new hairstyle sat atop her head like a helmet, with curls that cascaded onto her forehead and covered her glasses. Two young girls I had never seen before, who I later learned were her friends from the boarding school, circled Adella, examining every detail of her face, her hairdo, her dress, exclaiming with cries of exaggerated amazement over her manicure and her white shoes.

The sound of drumbeats intensified, announcing that the ceremony would soon begin, and, at that moment, as though she had been waiting for a signal from the drummer, a hand, which turned out to be my mother's, clamped down on the nape of my neck and pulled me backward. Then my Aunt Vika burst through the door to the room, carrying the bridal veil. I grabbed onto the doorframe with both hands, trying to twist out of my mother's grasp, and witnessed an astonishing sight. My aunt approached Adella, brandishing her hand as if she intended to slap her, but instead she tore Adella's glasses from her face, placed the veil in her hands, turned, pushed one of my hands off the doorframe and disappeared, leaving Adella sitting wide-eyed, her gaze roving. Apparently the shock was enough to cause my mother to loosen her grip on my neck.

"Give them back," Adella screamed, but my aunt had already been swallowed up in the crowd of guests, and the music roared and devoured her cry. At the sight of the tears pooling in her eyes, which now looked normal-size, one of the girls asked uncertainly, "Should I go and get them?"

"No," Adella conceded, breathing heavily. "She won't give them back."

I turned to my mother, "She can't see without her glasses."

"It's none of our business." My mother pulled me back to the table. I was being yanked along a couple of steps behind her, when the girl from the boarding school caught up with us, panting, and said, "The bride is asking for her bridesman." With no plausible reason to refuse, my mother unwillingly released my arm.

Adella called my name as I came toward her and when I answered she stretched out her arm in the direction of my voice. Despite the haircut and the wedding dress her countenance lacked even a trace of anticipation and bore only the same aggrieved expression as that first time at my grandfather's house. She ran her fingers over my face and said, "I saw you at the door before. Were you standing there for a long time?"

"I got there just before Aunt Vika."

"You saw what she did to me?"

"Yes."

She inclined her head to hear my "yes" clearly, perhaps searching for indignation and hostility in my voice.

"We will remember this," she said coldly, quietly, in a tone that frightened me, straightening her dress with both hands as her friend affixed the veil to her hair. "Do you see my collar?"

"Muga silk. Beautiful," I said.

Aunt Lily stood in the doorway holding two lit candles and said with pride, declaring, without actually uttering the words, that this wedding was taking place thanks to her, "*Yalla*, let's get married. The rabbi says to come, and the groom is ready and waiting."

Adella clutched my arm with one hand and the arm of one

of her two friends with the other, and Aunt Lily placed a candle in my free hand and another in the girl's free hand and said, "Hold them straight so that heaven forbid they don't set fire to something."

And that's how we started to move slowly toward the dais, the candle flames casting their light on the bride from either side.

"You are my eyes," said Adella as we walked. "I can't see a thing."

There were moments, during the celebration and especially on the walk toward the wedding canopy, when I imagined that I too could barely see, like Adella, as I traversed bright and luminous splashes of cloudlike shapes. The blazing bulbs and the mirrors on the walls beamed flashes of light into the fog that enveloped us and intermittently illuminated us as we sailed through the assembled guests, among blotches of color, Adella's right hand tightly gripping my arm. She leaned on me as she climbed the three steps to the little stage, blinded further by the flash of the photographer's camera as he stepped in front of her and aimed his lens. Uncle Moshe, his posture perfectly erect, stood opposite us wearing a festive suit, flanked by his father and his elder brother, and I imagined that she perceived him as a dark pillar, heard the voice of the rabbi, and directed her responses to the place from where the questions emanated. The band fell silent when Adella stood before her groom and he extended his arm to cover her face with the veil. I stood there, tense, my entire being focused on serving as her eyes, unaware of the candle being taken from my hand. Occasionally I stretched up on tiptoe and whispered the sequence of events into her ear. "Now Uncle Moshe is taking out the ring . . . Now the rabbi is reading from the page . . . Take the page from Uncle Moshe . . . Now the rabbi is blessing the wine . . . Now you have to drink . . . Now he's going to break the glass." And then almost at the same moment came the sounds of the crunch of breaking glass and the groom's sigh of relief followed by a chorus of *mazel tov* and a roar of applause. Adella grabbed my hand and said, "Bring me to the table and get my glasses from your aunt."

"Two more steps and then we go down three stairs." I led her to the decorated family table. Once she was seated I turned to Aunt Vika and asked for the glasses, but she adamantly refused, and at that moment my mother's hand reappeared and snatched me away, propelling me to my seat.

From across the huge expanse of table I observed Adella and my Uncle Moshe. They sat next to each other like two strangers, looking off to the side in embarrassment, not speaking, as though they had never had that heart-to-heart conversation in Yarden's sunny room. Suddenly I was fraught with worry. If my father and mother, who had married for love, as their honeymoon photos attested, argued constantly, how could the relationship between these two, who had been artificially affixed to one another, possibly succeed, united as they were by only their disabilities and their misery? I regretted that I hadn't managed to tell Adella that for the entire month, ever since she had revealed to me the contents of her suitcase, I had dreamed of the fabrics she showed me, that I remembered every detail of what she had taught me, that the textures of the swaths of material still tingled in my fingertips, and that all that I desired was to kneel once again before her suitcase of wonders and study the notebooks page by page. If only her eyes had the power to see, she would have perceived the yearning in mine, the shadow of my apology for believing for even a fleeting instant that she was dangerous and malicious.

When the guests started to leave I went over to Aunt Vika. "Grandfather says you should give her back her glasses," I lied. She hesitated for a moment, looked around to make sure that the hall was emptying out and without a word extracted them from a pocket in her purse and handed them to me, squeezing them tightly in her fist in one last effort to cause harm.

I went over to Adella and placed the glasses in her palm.

"Today I was supposed to be a queen." She put on her glasses and swiveled her head to survey the hall.

"Now she gives them to me, only now, when all the guests are gone. You should have managed to get them from her sooner. Some bridesman." Her wide eyes took in the size of the hall and the dais with the shiny white canopy, the desolate tables littered with leftover food and wine stains, the small number of relatives still milling around, Moshe sitting beside her, and finally they settled on the hurt in my face.

"What, you're mad at me? My mother wouldn't let me move."

She studied my face and replied, "I shouldn't be mad at you, I should be mad at the person who took my glasses. Because until now I couldn't see your beautiful tie."

"I asked her why she took them. She said she wanted you to look pretty."

"You should have asked her if it was more important to me, to look pretty. She made me blind at my own wedding."

"It's too bad," I said. "You would have seen in the mirror that your collar was the most beautiful collar of all."

And that was the only moment during her wedding when Adella laughed.

On the Saturday night after the wedding, when the newly-weds were still in Tel Aviv for the last day of their honeymoon, my Uncle Menashe told everyone about what happened when he drove them to the hotel. Uncle Menashe was a morose person who looked constantly anxious. I once heard my mother say that if it wasn't for the excellent challah breads he baked not a customer would have set foot in his store because they would have taken one look at his gloomy face and backed out of the bakery. But on that Saturday Menashe was as merry as someone who had had too much to drink. The story he related was accompanied by sweeping gestures and once he even stood up to imitate Uncle Moshe's posture. With that uncharacteristic joviality, unable to contain his mirth, he described how Adella and Moshe had sat in silence in the backseat of his car, how they had frozen in shock at the sight of the giant revolving door at the entrance to the luxurious hotel, how they climbed out of the car totally bewildered and still couldn't bring themselves to look at each other, how they took the two new identical suitcases and pulled them over to the revolving door where they stood stock still before the spinning glass until the doorman hurried toward them. Menashe, who was watching all this from the driver's seat, he gleefully recounted, saw how they were expelled into the grand lobby, practically tripping over one another. Then the doorman led them to the reception desk where they stood for a long time until Moshe unzipped the front pocket of his suitcase, withdrew a piece of paper and handed it to the clerk. A young man and woman dressed in white, also guests of the hotel, arrived and approached a second clerk, and the two couples stood side by side at the counter and also turned away at the same moment. Menashe watched as the clerk who had taken care of Adella and Moshe gestured to a uniformed porter who quickly walked over to take the two cases and lead them to the elevator. As they waited there the couple in white came over, hand in hand, and stood alongside Adella and Moshe. Menashe then told his spellbound audience—and at this point he was shaking with laughter—that Adella looked over at the young couple, particularly at the way their fingers were entwined and immediately reached out her hand to Moshe's and held it in exactly the same way. Two couples, each one holding hands, disappeared into the elevator along with the uniformed porter. And then Menashe drove off.

Yosef's wife, who was sitting next to her husband at the end of the table, said something that I couldn't catch, and for a moment it was as if there was a sudden, shared intake of breath

among all the people sitting there, followed by an elusive mur-
mur which circulated from mouths to ears, and some people
began to chuckle and then to giggle in an embarrassed way,
trying to stifle the sounds, fighting in vain against the waves rising from their bellies until the half-strangled merriment forged
a path to shaking shoulders and heads lowered to the tabletop.
The laughter gradually increased in momentum until it issued
from throats, and as more people yielded to their amusement
they ignited the glee of the others around the table. The more
they tried to hush their laughter, the more they endeavored to
rein it in, the more it burst forth, almost reaching a crescendo,
until someone let out a large groan which put paid to any remaining efforts at restraint, and the others joined in, their
bodies convulsing first with hilarity and then with the effort to
contain it. Esther, who was sitting opposite me, folded her arms
on the table and let her head drop onto them, two ample fans
of wrinkled white flesh vibrating above her elbows. At that moment, when it seemed the noise was dying down, Lily emitted a
lusty drawn-out squeal and the others joined her in a chorus of
screams, and then the shriek of a chair being pushed back rose
above the ruckus, followed by a thud as Yosef's wife dropped to
the floor and stayed there, still rocking with laughter, until her
husband and her sister hurried over to help her up.

I gaped in astonishment at the group of madmen. I had
never seen them so out of control, banging on the table with
their fists, wiping the tears from their eyes, moaning and clutching their sides.

"Why are you laughing?" I shouted to be heard over the
tumult.

My Uncle Yosef stopped short and looked at me.

"You get out of here. Go to the other kids!" he shouted and
then burst into laughter again.

"Why were you laughing like a bunch of crazy people?" I
asked my mother the following day.

"You shouldn't speak that way about your aunts and uncles."

"So why were they laughing not like a bunch of crazy people?"

"You wouldn't understand," she said with a mischievous smile, clearly amused at the memory of whatever it was.

"Were you laughing at Adella and Moshe?"

"Enough with the questions," but she still had that smile plastered on her face.

I waited for Adella to come back from the honeymoon. I knew that the day before the wedding she had transferred her belongings—and the suitcase with the fabric must have been among them—to my grandfather's home. I planned to give her a few days to adjust to her new life and then show up there on the pretext of visiting my grandfather, and ask her to show me the contents of the suitcase into which I had only had a peek. But my mother forbade me to go to my grandfather's house without her, and our visits always coincided with the times when Adella wasn't at home. She also invented all sorts of excuses not to attend the Saturday-evening gatherings. Still, if they talked about something important on those evenings when she was absent she compensated with visits to her sisters during the week and with phone calls. Rina, Lily's daughter, the one who was having trouble becoming pregnant, had visited the grave of the sage Rabbi Shimon Bar Yochai, hoping he would intercede; my cousin Yiftach, who was serving in the IDF, Menashe's son, the one who was injured in a training accident, lost his foot when the doctors couldn't save it; Esther had started her Pesach cleaning even before the Purim holiday.

"Why am I not allowed to visit Grandpa by myself?" I asked my mother a month after the wedding.

"Because you don't want to visit Grandpa. We know who you want to visit," she wouldn't even utter her name.

"And why am I not allowed to see Adella?"

"Because she's a bad influence on you."

"She teaches me about fabrics. It interests me. We can do it next to Grandpa, we won't be alone."

"What do you care about fabrics? They're for girls. What are you planning to be? A seamstress? You should start studying for junior high."

"Junior high is a year away."

"A year is not a long time. If you want to get into a good school, you'd better start studying now."

"Why do you hate her so much?"

"I don't hate her. She doesn't exist for me. When you give someone your heart, you give them good wine, and in return they give you vinegar—that's unforgivable."

My mother, whose kindness and generosity I had known since I was a child, was able to harden her heart irrevocably if she believed that her goodness had been abused.

I searched for other routes to Adella. And the more difficult it was, the more I yearned for her, for her musical voice, her mysteriousness, her suitcase of wonders, to know how she was spending her days and especially her nights. To sneak into my grandfather's house in defiance of my mother's prohibition was dangerous. My Uncle Moshe, who could never tell a lie, would give me away in a heartbeat. In the end I decided to phone her, to make do with the sound of her voice. Sometimes she would say, "Sorry, wrong number," and slam down the receiver. I wasn't dissuaded by these incidents. I would phone again from different public phones, and again she would hang up on me, but once in a while I would phone when she was alone in the guestroom, where the phone was, and then we would talk, hurrying to ask and answer and tell each other things. She would apologize for hanging up on me, explaining that my grandfather or my uncle had been close by, and the phone was attached to the wall. My grandfather believed that cordless phones were unreliable. And besides, she couldn't talk to me in their presence. And then I would ask how she spent her days, not daring to inquire into her nights. She would answer briefly that she did what she had to do, and then ask me what I had learned at school that day. Once I told her about the Bermuda Triangle, a region in the North Atlantic Ocean, not far from Florida, I explained, telling her that planes which fly over it and ships which enter its area are sometimes swallowed up or disappear without a trace, and some scientists think there may be a magnetic force which pulls metals toward it and causes them to plunge into the sea. Another time I talked about what I learned about how salmon swim against the current all the way back to the stream where they were born to lay their eggs and ensure their survival. She was excited by what I told her, would consider it and make observations and promise to tell Uncle Moshe about such interesting phenomena. Sometimes she would tell me about her daily routine. One time I asked if she could teach me about the fabrics over the telephone but she insisted that there was no point if I couldn't touch them. "It would be like kissing over the phone," she said. Afterwards I would replay the conversation in my memory from the first sentence to the last, delving for details she hadn't explicitly provided, wondering about her nights and her responses to my cautious questions about whether she was happy in her new life. Her voice gave nothing away. She sounded neither happy nor miserable, neither enthusiastic nor apathetic, as if trying to elude me, to erase from her voice any signs of sadness or joy.

I eagerly awaited the wedding of my cousin Tamar, Vika's eldest daughter, where I would see Adella even if I wouldn't be able to talk to her. But just two days before the wedding Uncle Moshe was rushed to hospital because of a problem with his heart, and Adella remained there by his side. I only found out at the wedding itself.

"Who are you waiting for so anxiously?" My mother feigned ignorance as she smoothed the folds of her dress.

"For Uncle Moshe," I replied.

And then she told me that he had undergone a cardiac catheterization, watching me like a hawk for the signs of disappointment.

"So we'd better go visit him," I suggested with alacrity.

"I'll visit him for you. You have too much to do with your math and your English lessons."

Four times a week I attended private math and English lessons in an effort to improve my average and my chances of being accepted by the new, most in-demand school in the city. In the phone calls from Los Angeles my father urged me to study hard. Now he asked to talk to me after every conversation with my mother, and he would tell me a little about Los Angeles, about the business he was building, about how he wasn't permitted to leave the U.S. until he had his Green Card, and that was why he hadn't attended his brother-in-law Moshe's wedding. My mother would hover over me during these conversations, her ears peeled, hearing his lies, most likely realizing that I was becoming closer to my father.

"What were you laughing about?" she asked after one of those calls.

"He told me he could see a squirrel hopping in the garden."

"What does he know. It was probably a cat," she dismissed him.

"Must have been a cat," I agreed loyally.

And then came the rainy days, and the evenings were shorter, and I became immersed in my studies and my new friendship with Daniel, a boy from a Russian family. Our English teacher put us together because we were at the same level and we both wanted to get into the new junior high.

Once, when Daniel and I were on our way back from an English lesson, I suddenly saw Adella in the distance, waiting at the bus stop, wearing a brightly colored sweater similar to the one she had shown me on the day when she revealed the contents of her suitcase. At the time I had called it "a sweater from an enchanted kingdom," I remembered with a snort, while now it seemed embarrassingly overdone. Although the bench was empty she preferred to stand, resting her weight on her good leg, her head lowered as she rummaged in her bag.

I was so shocked that I froze. In the end, my mother had managed to drive a wedge between us. I was swept up in my life, and in any case the family gatherings had moved from the house of my ailing grandfather to the siblings' homes, and I had long stopped attending them, showing up only at my mother's command for Rosh Hashana and the Pesach Seder. We rarely spoke on the phone anymore. Daniel and his friends had taken the place of Adella and Uncle Moshe and the others.

And in any case, until then I had only seen Adella inside. I had never encountered her in the street or seen how pathetic she appeared in the light of day. I was afraid that she would raise her head and see me and then I would have to cross the road and maybe even introduce her to Daniel. I quickly matched his stride and continued walking, hiding behind him when we passed the bus stop, relieved when the bus pulled up and blocked us from view. I didn't dare turn around to check whether she was still standing there or had boarded the bus. It crossed my mind that she might have seen me first and only pretended to be searching for something in her bag. After that I never phoned her again.

For the next two years I was engrossed in my schoolwork, in Daniel's band and in short and painful crushes on the girls in my class at the new junior high. Daniel and I had both been accepted, and we always sat together. I spent my Fridays with him and his group of friends. I would see Adella on the holidays, at family celebrations, or at times of grief like the seven-day *shivah* period of mourning after my grandfather died, but the mortifying image of her standing at the bus stop, dressed like a clown, her head buried inside her bag, had eradicated any desire to meet her. From the fragments of sentences that reached me I understood that in the end Uncle Yosef had his way, and several times a week Adella worked under him at his store for a puny salary. On Thursdays and Fridays she rose at four in the morning to prepare special cakes at Menashe's bakery, and as the demand for her delicious baking increased she was further enslaved to her work there. My uncles started sending her to the bakery on Saturday evenings as well to prepare the rolls for baking on Sunday morning, so that in any case she was absent from most of the dwindling family get-togethers.

At first these descriptions broke my heart, but by now I felt just a pinch of stinging embarrassment, a feeble remnant of my previous indignation at injustice. At those family gatherings that she did attend, Adella would look over at me from the other end of the room with puzzled eyes, which I would try to evade. Once she even approached me and revealed her annoyance: "Why don't you come to visit your uncle?" And once she risked the question, "You don't want to see the fabrics in the suitcase anymore?" But as far as I was concerned Adella and her suitcase belonged to an earlier period of my life, to my childhood, which I regarded from a new vantage point as I drew a razor across my nascent beard, occasionally drank beer directly from the bottle, hid magazines with pictures of naked women under my mattress, and cast surreptitious glances at the bodies of strange women in the street, imagining the breasts and crotches concealed by their clothing. By now I was living a different life where there was no room for Adella and my uncles and aunts. Even my cousins, who just a few years before had been the center of my life, receded from the heart of the family toward their own lives.

Also during those months my father and his brother started to import dried fruits and spices. His name was whispered around the tables at the family celebrations. By chance I overheard something about some complications with the income-tax authorities in Israel and a threat of a court case and even imprisonment if he returned. From their phone calls I learned that my mother was blaming my final years of high school and the mandatory army service that would follow for our delay in joining him. Their conversations became less frequent, and when they did take place they were brief and left me on the verge of tears. In the meantime, my elder brother Rafi finished his extra service in the army and joined my father to help with the business. My sister Yarden would complete her studies at the College of Education, Technology, and Arts by the end of the year and was planning to get married. But it seemed that she and her future husband were also considering moving to Los Angeles to join the family business that required more helping hands, preferably those attached to relatives.

I listened to my mother's conversations, and I heard her impatience, her constant complaints, and her displeasure at the fact that her two adult children had decided to join my father. The house was as neat and tidy as before, and meals were always prepared, but my mother's good and generous spirits had waned. She was less strict with me about my schoolwork and became accustomed to the lateness of my homecomings on Friday nights. Sometimes I would find her sitting alone facing the television, gazing at the screen, and it was clear that her thoughts were elsewhere.

And one day, probably owing to a rumor that had reached her, my mother uttered a sentence rife with portent disguised as a casual remark. "You know, now that the Gulf War is over, maybe I'll join your father, and you'll stay with Aunt Lily."

"For how long?"

"I don't know yet. It's hard for your father to be there alone. He needs help. And in any case in two months you'll have finished junior high and it will be summer vacation."

"About how long?"

"Maybe a few weeks . . ."

"A few weeks?!"

"It all depends on your father's situation."

"I don't like Aunt Lily."

"She lives the closest to your school."

"I can stay at home by myself."

"You can't."

"So send me to a boarding school."

"Stop talking nonsense." She slapped the back of my hand, shocked at the very thought. "You're not an orphan. And Aunt Lily loves you."

At Aunt Lily's house I was assigned the room of my cousin Yair, who studied at the Israel Institute of Technology in Haifa and rarely came home, and when he did I slept on the sofa in the lounge. On the shelves above his bed stood rows upon rows of model airplanes. At night, when I couldn't sleep, I imagined earthquakes which toppled the planes onto my head. I would wake up with bloodshot eyes to the sound of the alarm clock and feel confused all day long.

My longings for my mother started during the second week after she flew. During our first telephone call I couldn't hold back my tears. Aunt Lily grabbed the phone out of my hand and said, "I don't know what got into him. Until now he was perfectly normal."

At night, in Yair's bed, to my surprise I dreamed of Adella. Not of the pathetic Adella I encountered at the family affairs, but of Adella on the day when she arrived for her first meeting with Uncle Moshe, and of Adella when she sat across from my uncle in my sister's room. By morning the dream would have faded, but I knew that she had been there in my bed, her hair spread across the pillow, her body soft as a nymph's, crushing her breasts against my chest, arousing me, pressing into me, smelling like flowers. The disturbing thought lodged in my mind that it was Yair who had dreamed about her, and when he moved, had left her there in his bed. Once the surprise had worn off, I began to take pleasure in the remnants of the dream, the heat of her breasts in the palms of my hands, my trembling fingers as they travelled up the interior of her thighs. Sometimes an image of Adella would fill my mind when I was daydreaming in class, or during conversations with one of the groupies who followed Daniel's band. And so I would lie in Yair's bed and hope for more dreams about Adella, on some mornings remembering the electricity that coursed through me when my dream Adella brought her lips to mine.

I wondered if any of my cousins, who started adolescence when I did, also dreamed about her. Some of them were already occupied with their compulsory army service and preferred to spend their free time with their friends; some were busy studying for end-of-year exams. My younger cousins were still exiled to the spare bedroom, but there weren't many of them, and they were surprisingly quiet.

At one of the gatherings which took place at my Aunt Lily's, Adella and my Uncle Moshe were also there. Seeing them made me feel guilty about my dreams, and I silently apologized to them both. Adella sat by her husband at the table, her head bowed, silent, and there was no resemblance between her and the sensuous woman I saw in my sleep. Occasionally she would tilt her head toward her husband's and whisper to him, and then her glasses would touch his face. I recalled my fear that maybe she had seen me first on that day when I pretended not to see her standing at the bus stop. But the two of them never even looked my way, just sat like neglected guests at the end of the table, far from the talkative family circle.

Confronted with the sight of them, the feeling that had pulsed within me five years previously was rekindled. A sense of the injustice inflicted on the weak Adella by my powerful aunts and uncles. I went over and crouched behind them, and they were surprised and moved apart so I could sit between them.

"How you've grown." Adella's eyes glowed in her pale face. From up close I saw that her hair was cut short and straight, unlike the soft loose hair of the woman in my dreams. "Right, he's grown, Moshe? Look at him."

"Gulliver," said Uncle Moshe and we all laughed.

"What does your mother say?" asked Adella. "How long will she be in America?"

"She doesn't know."

"But your Aunt Lily is treating you well," Adella said, soothingly, twisting her upper body to face me, and in my imagination the top of her dress slipped down, exposing her soft breasts.

"But she doesn't make delicious cakes for you, like Adella's," Uncle Moshe whispered into my ear, as if fearful of being overheard. "Come visit and see what kind of cake you'll get."

I sensed a quiet, shared serenity between Adella and my Uncle Moshe, and I thought about it again at the end of the evening, when everyone had left, a tranquil fondness and mutual respect which was absent from my parents' relationship.

"What did you talk about with Adella?" my Aunt Lily demanded to know the next day before I left for school.

"Uncle Moshe invited me to visit them for cake."

"Your mother says you aren't allowed to."

"She didn't tell me that I'm not allowed to."

"She told me."

"Why?"

"Because it's not Uncle Moshe you want to visit. And there are things about her that you don't know," as if it wasn't she herself who had brought Adella into the family.

"I know that she works for free for Uncle Yosef and Uncle Menashe."

"She doesn't work for free, if you must know. She works in exchange for their rent. Ever since Grandfather died. It isn't their apartment: it belongs to all the siblings. And Yosef keeps her on a short leash. He doesn't let her lift up her head. If he did—she would bite him."

Suddenly I felt dizzy.

"What's wrong with you?" my aunt could tell something wasn't right. "Do you feel sick? Did you catch something?"

"I'm fine."

"Maybe you should stay home today?"

"I can't. I have my last exam."

"Good luck," she kissed the top of my head. "You're our most talented boy. Go and do well, then we'll tell your mother the good news."

I answered the questions on my history exam from deep within a fog. I dragged my hand across the test paper with difficulty, the letters dancing before my eyes growing larger and then smaller or flying off the page as if they weren't anchored there and the slightest puff of wind could blow them away. Some part of my consciousness remained unclouded. I understood the questions and I knew the answers, but it was hard for me to transfer the information from my mind to the page.

The teacher looked at me when I stood to hand in the exam and placed her hand on my forehead.

"You've got a fever, you're burning up!" she cried. "Why didn't you say something?" She made me sit down on a chair next to her, and one of the other students was sent to bring me water from the Teachers' Room. Black spots danced before my eyes, dazzled by the sun shining through the classroom windows. The gym teacher was commandeered to drive me home in her car. "What's the address?" she asked as she pushed the seat next to her into a reclining position. Lying there with my eyes closed I gave her Adella's address, and for the entire journey I plummeted toward an ever-receding piece of ground.

"He has a temperature, you have to call the doctor," the gym teacher announced as she shepherded me into the house. "Where's his bed?"

And then everything misted over. Later I learned that the doctor was called, an injection was administered, a nurse was summoned to take blood samples, and medicine was purchased. My fever raged for the entire night. In the morning I wasn't sure whether I was awake or dreaming, dead or alive. Adella sat at my bedside, awash in the sunlight that poured through the window, holding a damp cloth which she was using to wipe my brow.

"You'll be fine," she said. "I made you soup. In a little while you'll eat."

"Am I alive?" I croaked.

"Of course. You're at your Uncle Moshe's house."

"I want to stay here," I said and I closed my eyes, inhaling the scent of Adella as she leaned over me.

"I want you to, too," she whispered.

Later I learned that Aunt Lily had done her best to relocate me to Yair's room at her house, but the doctor informed her that if I left my bed it would only be to go to the hospital, and my Uncle Yosef decided to heed the doctor's words and leave me at Moshe and Adella's. For days and nights at a stretch Adella stayed by my side, and for three weeks she was absent from her various jobs at my uncles' businesses. Five days after I collapsed my mother came back, and the two women took it in turns to look after me. As if from a distance I heard my mother talking about the end of apartheid in South Africa and how Berlin had replaced Bonn as the German capital. After that, between waves of dizziness and chills, I saw only my mother.

For two weeks I lay in bed, most of the time half-asleep, in a daze. When my fever finally broke and the doctor allowed it, I left for Los Angeles with my mother. For the entire flight I had daydreams of scenes from the nature channel. I saw a pride of lions loping across the arid plains of Africa; starbursts exploding in the velvety black heavens until the skies emptied; a bird's-eye-view panorama of ripples of water burbling from the depths, oscillating and expanding to the edges of time; a stormy night when brilliant flashes of lightning tore across the sky in zigzag patterns; undersea plants undulating like dancers among white corals; flocks of flamingos with erect pink necks.

Among the nature images floated Adella's face, smiling and melancholy, surprised and hurt, coming closer and retreating, shrinking to a pinpoint and suddenly expanding and approaching, so near that it was out of focus, and then her lips would touch mine with a jolt of electricity.

PART TWO
ADEL

The closer the plane gets to Israel the more urgently I ponder the question: Did Adella really learn about my career as a ghostwriter after she came across my website? Did she really imply that she was summoning me to tell me the story of her life? What part of that story merited being written? Maybe she wanted to document her years at the boarding school? Or the years before? Did she want to publicly condemn my aunts and uncles for the injustices they wrought, to describe how they married her to a disabled man twice her age? Did they still dominate her, force her to work for them for a pittance, defraying the cost of the rent she and Uncle Moshe had to pay; in my mother's words, "exploiting her like a slave?"

Or perhaps the reason is something altogether different, and she thinks I would be happy to take a break from my Los Angeles suburb. Did someone tell her that I had moved out?

None of those possibilities explain it, I conclude. So why, then, has she invited me now? Am I to be a conduit for a demand from the members of my family? And why did I accept her invitation? I wonder at my willingness to come. We could easily have dealt with any matter online. And if Adella was seeking a mediator between herself and my family, I am certainly not the right person.

I try to calculate her age and am surprised to conclude that she is forty-eight, am curious to know how the years have treated the young woman I can still picture, who was all of twenty-four when, burning with fever, I was delivered to her home by the gym teacher after my final exam at junior high.

I still remember my aunts and uncles, some of whom I am shocked to realize must be over eighty, and I don't even know whether they are dead or alive. I also acknowledge that I have forgotten the names of several of my younger cousins and more far-flung relatives, distant cousins of my mother's and their children. Behind closed eyelids I can retrieve childhood memories from those Saturday-evening gatherings at my grandfather's house and place them alongside the photographs in the family album that my mother still has among her possessions at the Blue Horizon facility for Alzheimer's patients and sits on the table covered with the cloth embroidered by my grandmother.

So great was my love for America, I justify this stupendous loss of memory, so deep my yearning to be from there, to excel as a player on the Whitney High School baseball team, and later to earn the title of team captain, to adopt the language and the accent as if not only me but also my parents had been born there, that I was compelled, it seemed, to entirely erase small details and large events so as to be reborn in Los Angeles. My world was soon filled with new people, and the severing of ties with my relatives, which my mother decreed for herself, made things easier for me.

I suddenly feel like an elderly man, trying to travel twenty years back in time, to breach the memories of childhood assaulting me in gusts of scent. The floral scents of the women's perfume, the hot, sweet aroma of baked goods piled on brass platters, the dusty smell of a house where the windows are kept closed, which pervaded my grandparents' home during the final months of my grandmother's life.

Images from the evening when I first saw Adella appeared in my mind during the flight, followed by a fragmented chain of events leading up to her wedding night when—my heart plunges at the memory—my Aunt Vika extended her arm and

grabbed Adella's glasses off her face, leaving her staring wide-
eyed into space, virtually blind. I feel my body unraveling and
suddenly recall my illness during the last two weeks of my life
in Israel, a sickness my mother diagnosed as a longing for her,
an anguished cry to bring her back sooner and to take me with
her the next time, while for her part she was coming to the realization that there was no life for her beyond Los Angeles, where
two of her three children were already putting down roots.

On that last visit my mother asked her siblings if they would
give her the tablecloth embroidered by their mother that was
handed from sister to sister and always adorned the festive Rosh
Hashana table. They conferred with one another, and only on
the day of her flight did they grant their consent, moving my
mother to grateful tears. She refused to be parted from it and
consign it to the cargo hold, clutching it in her lap for the entire
journey. The combined weight of our possessions along with
the tablecloth, which was packed in a separate suitcase, was
more than we were permitted to carry, and following prolonged
negotiations with the airline representative my mother left the
empty suitcase by the counter and carried the tablecloth in her
arms. From the gate we walked to the plane together, my mother
supporting me as I tried not to lean on her too heavily, and she
hoisted her hand luggage and then sat in her seat clutching the
tablecloth in both hands.

When we were seated she spread it over her lap, and in her
sleep she caressed the embroidered peacock feathers.

For that first year my mother was physically present in Los
Angeles, but her true being remained at her siblings' homes, as
she spoke to her sisters once a week and wrote them frequent
letters. She would recount the latest family news to us, repeat-
ing the details as we sat around the Shabbat table on Friday
nights, endeavoring to connect the threads of longing for family that extended across two continents. Rina, Lily's daughter,
gave birth to twins; Lily's son received his license to practice

medicine; Uncle Yosef suffered a heart ailment, underwent surgery, and immediately returned to work at his clothing store; Esther's son divorced his gentile wife and returned to live in Israel; Menashe's son with the amputated foot won sports competitions for the disabled; Adella was pregnant, and Moshe fussed around her all day, unable to contain his joy.

Right after the Friday-night meal my friend Michael would come to pick me up, and we would usually go to hear a local band perform at a rock concert. Going out on Shabbat, which was expressly forbidden when we lived in Israel, was grudgingly tolerated with a defeated scowl in Los Angeles. Because the distances between places were so much greater there, my brother and sister had commenced the battle over the prohibition against travel on Shabbat before I joined them. And my parents, visibly reluctant, had no choice but to allow us to learn how to fit in in the new country they had imposed upon us. On the way to the concert I found myself preoccupied with Adella's pregnancy. I wondered how she would manage with her bad leg, and what the chances were that the baby would inherit its parents' disabilities. Perhaps my aunts would be kinder to her, now that she was about to become a mother. Would they be nice to her and help her out, as they helped the other pregnant women in the family? When Michael and I met up with our friends those musings were pushed to the back of my mind, and after that I barely spared a thought for Adella's pregnancy as she and my uncles and aunts were crowded out of my thoughts by the stimulating events of my new life.

At that time my mother still didn't know what she would learn several months later, and until then had been no more than a rumor. My father had not managed to remain faithful to her during the years he had spent alone in Los Angeles. There were women in his life, and one of them, an American woman who worked at his store, had even given birth to his daughter. Since our Iranian community revolved around one synagogue, and most of the members knew each other, many people were aware of the relationship, even though my father never appeared in public with the woman. When my mother learned of it, she also found out that when the baby was born her siblings in Israel had heard the news, and instead of intervening on behalf of their sister and telling her adult children about their father's deeds so as to distance them from him, or urging her to join her husband and save her family, they had done nothing and not divulged a word. She never forgave them for their betrayal, stopped phoning them and writing to them, and no pleading letters or imploring phone calls or messengers sent to appease her made the slightest difference. My mother was not blessed with the gift of forgiveness, and in one fell swoop all contact between them was cut. My siblings and I were entirely consumed by our new worlds, and her decision made it easier for us to disconnect from our old homeland.

It was just a few years after the shock of the knowledge that her husband never stopped seeing the American woman or supporting her and their daughter that the initial signs of my mother's Alzheimer's appeared. At first it was easy to dismiss them as difficulties with a new language or cultural differences. But when she barged into one of the houses on our street insisting that it was hers and attacked the woman who lived there, who immediately called the police, who in turn involved the welfare authorities, there was no escaping the truth. The disease progressed quickly, and one of its manifestations was violent behavior toward people she didn't recognize who came into our house, one of whom was a girl in my class who never spoke to me again. Finally—I was already away at college—when no carer could be found who was willing to stay with her, my father had no choice but to move her to a reputable institution, the Blue Horizon, and that used up the last of the money left over from the sale of the apartment in Israel. In that way my father salved his conscience regarding the woman and her daughter, with whom he was always in touch. One time when I was visiting my mother, in a rare moment of lucidity which penetrated the fog in her brain, she told me that she had known about the woman in my father's life from the first night he slept with her. My grandmother had come in a dream to tell her about it, she said, but her hands were tied in those days. She had two children serving in the army, one nearing the end of his service while the other had just been inducted, and also me, a nine-year-old boy.

Images from the past flicker beneath my closed eyelids, presenting me with a riddle which teasingly vanishes before I can contemplate it. A flight attendant leans over me, offering champagne, and I sip the drink, causing the pictures to whir past more quickly. My grandfather rests his open palm on the top of my head; a row of model airplanes are lined up on a shelf above my cousin's bed; the nightlight glows in Yarden's bedroom; a platter in a kitchen is stacked with pinwheel cookies; Daniel and his musician friends disappear from my life; the toiletries in my mother's bathroom are lined up according to height; I feel the electrifying texture of Muga silk.

And as the images fly by the question keeps hammering at my brain like the soundtrack of a ticking clock—why did Adella ask me to come?

Why is it so important to her that she even seduced me with a Business Class flight, and threw in a personal driver? Did she clean out her savings for this? Does she even have any savings? Did she take out a loan?

And then, with the effervescent champagne still tickling my senses, I hear the pilot announce that he is commencing our descent.

Business Class passengers disembark first, but I still have time to catch the news broadcast on the plane's screens showing the swearing-in ceremony of the members of Israel's Eleventh

Knesset, the parliament of the country I traded for another. I am swept up in the small group proceeding along the gangway until we reach the airport, and I stop in my tracks at the sight of the glass wall that encloses a brightly lit area with a fountain at its center ringed by tables and chairs, which are in turn encircled by a wide array of stores.

A vague memory of the old airport comes to mind: narrow, cramped. My mother and I sent off our luggage, abandoned the empty suitcase at the airline counter where I left the wheelchair, and with her supporting me we made for the escalator. At the bottom of that looping chain of linked steps we parted from the relatives who had come to escort us as far as the exit gate from the country. I still hadn't fully recovered, and the picture of my mother surrounded by her weeping siblings suddenly seems like the remnant of a dream. Uncle Menashe handed me a travel bag that he had been carrying, and I set it down near my mother, who was sobbing on the shoulder of her beloved sister Esther, and they all caressed the peacock tablecloth one last time before stepping back.

Returning to the present, still propelled by the stream of travelers which stops now at the baggage carousels, I notice an enormous advertisement on the wall facing me that reads, "El Al, Feel At Home, Away From Home," and I wonder with an unexpected pounding of my heart where my home is in this world. I was plucked from Israel too early, set down in Los Angeles at too mature an age to ever really "feel at home." My command of English is perfect, but when I fill in a questionnaire that includes a space for citizenship, I hesitate, if only for an instant. And then like all conmen I enter the word "American." Recognizing my suitcase, I lift it off the revolving belt and walk toward Arrivals, astonished at the size of the place, scanning the people scattered around the hall displaying signs.

An exceptionally well-dressed driver in a suit and tie brandishes a placard bearing my name. As I approach him, he

welcomes me by doffing his cap and extending his arm to remove the handle of my suitcase from my grasp, then turns and
strides off as if leading the way for a delegation of dignitaries. The
vehicle he conducts me to is gleaming and spacious, upholstered
in leather and in pristine condition. I look around in wonder. I
hadn't expected a driver or a car like these. Actually, I reflect as
he closes my door for me, I had no idea what to expect.

"Please, where are you taking me?" I follow the driver's
movements as he buckles his seatbelt, wondering if he lives with
my uncle and his wife in their old apartment.

"To Mrs. Adel."

"Adel? You must mean Adella?"

"I know her as Adel."

"I think you must be mistaken."

"I am not mistaken, sir. Her name is Adel."

"Have you known her a long time?"

"Fifteen years, give or take."

"In what capacity?"

"As her driver."

"Her driver?" I try to hide my bafflement.

"For her and for her customers."

I sit up straight in my seat.

"I think there has been a mistake. I think you were meant to
pick up someone else."

"No, no sir. She's waiting for you."

"The woman who's waiting for me doesn't have customers
who travel with a private driver."

"She does, sir. I earn my living from them."

"What kind of customers does she have? I'm sure there has
been a mistake. I have to get to Adella, not Adel."

"She's the same woman, sir."

"Why are you so sure?"

"Because she told me that you would argue with me because
you would be sure that it was a mistake."

I lean back, confused, trying in vain to make sense of the strange situation, look out at the oleander plants that line the highway, barely recognize Tel Aviv, which is dense with sky-scrapers, and before I know it the car is floating silently through the city's streets, and then it pulls up outside the Dan Hotel.

"This is the place? You're sure?"

"Yes, sir."

What does Adella, now known as Adel, do in a hotel? Who are the clients who are ferried by the elegant driver? And what does any of this have to do with her bringing me here?

He hurries to get out of the car and in an instant is waiting politely for me on the sidewalk, his every movement the gesture of a faithful servant as he tilts the handle on my suitcase toward me. I pull out my wallet, and he stops me.

"Everything is paid for, sir. I hope you have a pleasant vacation in Israel. Mrs. Adel will meet you on the other side."

The revolving door expels me into the lobby of the luxurious hotel. Filling the space that separates me from the glass wall that reveals the sea are scattered tables, sofas, armchairs with people positioned among them like actors. Opposite the reception counter is a corridor tiled in white marble that leads to a row of very brightly lit shops. At the entrance to the third one I see an attractive woman wearing a purple skirt, her hair piled atop her head, leaning comfortably against the doorframe with her arms folded across her chest, smiling at me.

I stand there gazing at the woman who elicits not the slightest hint of recognition, while at the same time I know that she is Adella, and I wonder if not only the passage of time but also the aftereffects of the champagne are responsible for her transformation. So she conducts her business from here, and apparently that is how she became rich; she procures women for the hotel clients. People move about in the open space between us, unaware of the bolt of lightning that has just struck the man gripping the handle of his suitcase, who stands like a statue by the revolving door. A woman moves to survey the display window of the first shop in the row and blocks our view of one another. We are both standing perfectly still, allowing the first wave of shock to recede. After what feels like an eternity, Adella drops her arms and moves toward me, smiling.

"Hello Micha," a distant memory of her rich voice surfaces.

"Adella . . ."

"It's been Adel for a long time now," she beams. "But I will permit you to call me Adella. You and your uncle."

At the mention of my uncle my American identity is snatched away. Having no other to shield me, I find myself exposed like a snail denuded of its shell. For a fraction of a second I wonder if it is appropriate for us to embrace, something we have never done in the past. But she smooths over my hesitation, threading her arm through mine like the elderly do, and leads me over to the entrance to the store where she was standing. Walking beside her, I suddenly imagine us as bride and groom approaching our wedding canopy. And now we have arrived at the store, and I can see the word emblazoned on the large glass wall—Adel. So she has changed her name for professional reasons. If this is really Adella, she seems to have been cured of her disabilities. Her eyes are bare, not magnified by thick-lensed glasses, and she doesn't limp. Was this also accomplished for professional reasons?

A laugh escapes me as I search for the hidden camera. She grins broadly as if reading my mind, and steadily, with firm steps, guides me into the store, as if confirming that we are in a reality show. Once we cross the threshold a strange sensation assails me, a sense that although I am in a place where I have never been there is something familiar about it. My eyes are drawn to a sweater hanging inside a glass display case. I am sure that I have seen it before, but how can that be? I need a long interval to riffle through my memory until, with a start, I recognize it. It's the sweater shimmering with color that Adella showed me in my previous life, on the day when my mother brought me to see her, a short time before her wedding. It's the sweater she was wearing on that day when she was waiting at the bus stop and I pretended not to see her. Again, as though she can tell what I'm thinking, she whispers, "Yes, it's that sweater."

And that's the moment when I realize that everything in the store is a variation of that sweater. Hanging on racks, folded on shelves, displayed on mannequins with tilted chins on an upper floor. Shirts and sweaters and dresses and coats and jackets and scarves and bags, all blazing with color, overflowing with ribbons and buttons and beads, each one unique, and all of them reflections of the original model contemplating the store from the high perch in its glass box like a prehistoric woman surveying her many descendants. No, apparently there isn't any hidden camera after all.

"It's the sweater from the enchanted kingdom." The two words I haven't uttered in tandem to describe an item of apparel since all those years ago are rescued from oblivion. Does she use all this as a cover for some dubious activity?

"You're right," she smiles and rings a small bell, which summons a young girl from behind a curtain.

"Naama, this is Micha, my bridesman. We are going to the studio now." She tugs at my hand and says, "Come," as she walks toward the spiral staircase which leads to the upper floor. I watch the back of the woman as she ascends and remind myself in amazement that this is Adella. It seems that I remain there watching her for a while, as I am startled to hear a voice from above: "Come up, Micha."

She really does sell the sweaters and purses she makes, but I can't rid myself of the suspicion that the whole thing is a front for something else.

There's a tiny magical room up here, with a carpeted floor, three walls covered in wallpaper and the fourth a giant mirror which multiplies the lively walls and the standing lamp in the corner, transforms three armchairs into six, duplicates Adella as well who is sitting in one of the armchairs, and the table set with a bowl of fruit, a jug, glasses, a plate of cakes, and a dish of sugared almonds. My gaze lingers on the almonds.

Maybe she doesn't really traffic in women: I revise my first thought; maybe she changed her name to Adel because of the sweaters. I sit facing her, and it's as though I'm seeing a mirage. She somewhat resembles the Adella of my memories, but she is also very different from her. She observes me as though she's deciphering each fragment of my thoughts. Of all the possibilities that had run through my mind when I imagined meeting her again—and in one of them she was dressed in rags, on her hands and knees, scrubbing the floors of my Uncle Yosef's store—of all the potential scenarios that I had concocted, the vision of this woman sitting in the glamorous loft of a luxurious store is the most fantastic of all. Once more we sit in silence for a long time, as I try to link the images I remember from the past with the figure sitting before me. To connect the young woman with the soaking wet hair shrinking into an armchair to the perfectly-at-ease woman sitting regally in another armchair; the blind bride groping her way to her wedding canopy to the woman regarding me with a mysterious smile. I wonder whether she is comparing that nine-year-old boy to the American man seated opposite her. The boy whose mother kept him close, to the man he became.

"Hard to believe, no?" she speaks for me as well.

"Hard . . ."

"This isn't how you imagined it would be." She seems to be enjoying the astonishment that I'm clearly experiencing.

"No . . ." I finally abandon the notion of the female pimp.

"Life is full of surprises." She gives voice to what I have learned many times over helping people to write their autobiographies.

"True . . ."

"Things aren't always what they seem."

"Yes . . . what happened to your glasses?"

"Ah," her smile expands. "Finally you say a complete sentence, and I can tell that you still speak Hebrew as though you never left."

"I speak Hebrew with my siblings. I have friends who speak Hebrew. So what happened to your glasses?"

"I threw them in the trash after I had laser surgery."

"It suits you . . . You can see your eyes . . ."

"That's what you said then as well, and I never forgot." She triggers the memory of the first time we met, and I realize that the first thing I said to her was about her eyes.

"I remember that!"

"You were the person I most wanted to tell after the operation. But you disappeared into America . . . I also ordered special shoes that disguise my limp." She stretches out her legs and kicks off her shoes. From the outside they look the same, but inside the right shoe there's an elevated insert above the heel. I hadn't noticed anything from the few steps she had taken.

"That's great."

Not only has her appearance changed, but also the timbre of her sentences.

"And you've grown in the meantime . . . I heard you have a family . . ."

"Yes." I wonder if any rumors about me have reached her. "Twins."

"And a good wife?" No, apparently she hasn't heard, or maybe she's testing me, waiting to see how I respond.

". . . Yes . . ."

"Iranian?"

"No!"

"So it must have been hard for your mother?"

"My mother was in no state to understand what was going on when I got married."

"Ah," she breathed sorrowfully. "I heard something like that as well."

"Who did you hear from? No one from the family is in touch with us anymore."

"Our community has spies everywhere. I was sorry when I heard. Of all your aunts and uncles she was the only one who was on my side at the beginning. I never forgot that."

"But afterwards she was angry at you." I would never forget the expression on my mother's face when she came to pick me up on the day when I discovered the wonders of the fabrics lovingly stored in the suitcase.

"People who can be endlessly good can also feel anger deeply. But we forgave one another when you were sick. She stayed with me for two weeks. We talked a lot."

"I never knew that you talked. She stayed angry."

"True. In the end we argued because of you. We both wanted what was best for you but we disagreed . . . I thought it was too soon for you to travel, but she wanted to get back to your father . . ."

We fell silent again. My mother had never told me about their reconciliation. It seemed that I was missing many pieces of the story.

"Tell me about my uncle. How is he?" I feel as though I am choosing the starting point for her story and am suddenly gripped with the fear of what hasn't occurred to me till now. Perhaps he is no longer alive.

"You'll see him for yourself." In the interval between my panic and her response my heart seemed to stop, but her calm voice relaxes me. He's still alive.

"You had a good life together," I say, almost incredulously.

"There were very hard years, but not because of him. Because of his brothers and sisters."

"But you saw the family on your first visit."

"Certainly. Your Uncle Yosef loathed me on sight."

"Not only him. Almost all the women were against you."

"The women in your family have no power. They sat with the men as if their opinions were taken into account. But it was only the men who made decisions about the important things."

"You saw that?"

"I saw everything."

"From that first evening when it rained?"

"Of course."

"So why did you agree to join the family?"

"Because I had to. And besides, my mother came to me in a dream. And I saw the eyes of your Uncle Moshe."

"What did you see?"

"That things would be fine with him."

"You saw that you would be able to do what you wanted with him?"

"But with love," she didn't smile as I had expected her to. "I saw that he had the desire for love."

"In general, or for love with you?"

"With me, with me. His eyes told me. And you and your mother also gave me strength. If no one had been on my side I would have let it go. Even my mother in the dream would have understood. Your uncle couldn't stand up to his brothers and sisters, he was weaker than the women."

"You understood all that when you were eighteen?"

"At eighteen, after what happened to me when I was ten, I was already old."

Naama's voice travels up the stairs, and Adella goes down to help with a customer. I watch her closely and can discern the slightest tendency to favor her left foot. I can hear the entire conversation and am surprised at the unfamiliar tone in Adella's voice. It's a cunning combination of authority and seduction that seems to contradict everything I know about her.

Actually, the thought takes shapes in my mind, I don't really know her at all. How valid are the things I perceived in her when I was a child? And while that thought is drifting through my head I hear her talking and persuading her customer to buy a scarf as well. Today they're thirty percent off. The prices they quote sound very high to me. I calculate the amount in dollars and realize that the sweater's price is in the hundreds. When the woman leaves, before Adella has a chance to come back upstairs, another customer comes in and asks in Russian-accented English whether she can pay in hryvnias, which is apparently Ukrainian currency, and Adella instructs Naama to consult with the bank clerk about the exchange rate and returns to me.

"You're a good saleswoman." I can't disguise the surprise in my voice.

"I love women who love my clothes."

"Four hundred dollars for a sweater!"

"Some of the sweaters cost thousands of dollars." She grins at my shocked face.

"Thousands of dollars for a sweater?!"

"I have customers who want real pearls. Lots of them want fourteen-carat gold thread. One of my clients asked for diamond buttons."

"Diamonds on a sweater?"

She nods, still smiling. Apparently diamond-studded sweaters are the norm in Adel's world.

"Do you still make them yourself?"

"I design all of them, draw every last detail, and choose the colors, but I have seamstresses in the workroom." She gestures toward a mirror that is actually a cleverly disguised door. "And the girls at the boarding school also help out. I only sew the precious stones."

"Did you dream of having a store like this?" I am trying to connect Adel to Adella.

"For sure. It was my dream the entire time I was at the boarding school. The dream kept me going."

"When I left you were miles away from that dream."

"Back then, I was a slave to your uncles." My mother's comments about her from that time echo across the years.

"And you got away from them!" I declare to my mother as well.

"Elisha freed me," she says deliberately, observing me keenly.

"Tell me." My professional experience shows me the gateway to the heart of her life story, like a gold prospector whose metal detector starts to beep, indicating that the vein is nearby.

"It's a long story," she says slowly, seeming to ponder for an extended moment, biting her lips. "Do you have the energy now? Don't you want to eat something? Do you want coffee? Aren't you tired after your flight? I asked you to come so I could tell you, you know that. The first time we met you told me that you wanted to be a writer. You should know that all these years I've thought of you. Every time something special happened to me I would say to myself that I had to remember so one day I could tell Micha. Every time I ate an almond, I wondered if you still remember the taste . . . I never forgot you, and I talked about you often with your uncle. Every year on your birthday I would beam good wishes to Los Angeles and try to imagine what you were doing." She watches me as though the expression on my face will supply her with the answer on the spot, and I try to evade her piercing stare, hoping she doesn't intuit my embarrassment, because for twenty-four years I have scarcely thought of her at all.

"Why did you never try to find me for all those years?" She is practically whispering, and I am shocked. Her voice is like that of a rejected lover's from some old melodrama. Did she really expect me to try to look for her?

"Here I am now." I try to surmount this hurdle. "Tell me what has happened to you since I left." I recognize the tone of voice that replaces my regular voice when I'm with my clients. I can already sense how the story will be written and am beginning to organize it; I'm already translating the spoken words into lines of writing.

"Wow." She places one palm on each cheek, seeking to express something that escapes words. For so many years she has been longing to tell me. It's a story which she sometimes relates in tiny snippets to the girls from the boarding school. She has already mentioned that she stays in touch with the boarding school. After years of trying, she received permission to open a textile class there. In addition to that, twice a week in the afternoon there's a sewing and knitting workshop that's open to all the girls so that they can learn a skill and will always have a way to support themselves. They prepare the basis for the garments that is followed by the artistic needlework. Most of their work isn't up to par, especially that of the beginners, but the connection to the school is important to her. She goes there once a week, and before every holiday she fills Alex's car—Alex is the driver who picked me up at the airport—with gifts and candy, and goes there to give them the presents and a hug. Her success story is an inspiration for them, permission to dream. Nothing gives her more strength than the girls' shining eyes—except for her son, Elisha. She chose the name Elisha despite the family's protests. Her husband supported her. They wanted to name him after my grandfather, and she didn't want to, wanted to keep the child for herself. She will tell me about Elisha. There is so much to tell. A photograph? Yes, of course she has a picture of him, here it is.

I look at Elisha's face, and it's as though I am gazing into a mirror when I was his age. I suddenly realize how much I resemble Uncle Moshe: the shape of the head, the neatly combed hair, the wide smile. The way Elisha holds himself also seems familiar, the way he's leaning against the wall, folding his arms across his chest and angling his head to the side as if he's looking away from the sun. I want to observe the expression on his face more closely, the look in his eyes, but she snatches the photo away and tucks it back in her wallet.

"Any chance I'll meet Elisha?"

"He introduced me to a girl for the first time . . . I think it's serious . . ."

Her eyes widen and seek mine.

I know this moment well. Sometimes it happens at the first meeting, and sometimes it takes several meetings, long conversations making tentative progress while groping in the dark until suddenly it comes to me. Now is the time to hold back; I know that if I sit and wait things will begin to flow, and here they are already starting to compose themselves in a parallel language, the language of the book that I will write. I sometimes wondered even years after a book was written and printed about the exact element in the way someone told me his or her story that in retrospect revealed itself to me as the beating heart of a life. When was the moment when we understood that we were holding onto one another as we embarked on a journey to connect among the disparate elements that comprised the mystery of their life story? Now it seems to me that Adella looks frightened for some reason. What is it about my request to meet Elisha that triggers this turmoil in her? At times like this hidden doors sometimes fly open.

We could begin with her story—she hastens to reposition the spotlight that had briefly illuminated Elisha, and directs her gaze toward the entrance to the hotel as though she can see through walls—we can begin the story right here, in this hotel, where she stayed with Moshe on their honeymoon. Most of the time people aren't aware in real time of the events that will change their lives. The honeymoon has a connection to this store. Yes, yes, she knows that it sounds strange but that's when it all started. The revolving door I came through a short time ago, do I remember it? There's nothing special about it, an ordinary revolving door. But when she and Uncle Moshe left my Uncle Menashe's car at the entrance to the hotel on their wedding night, it was the first time that either of them had seen a door like it. They stood there with no idea how to enter through that glass butterfly until one of the hotel workers came out and guided them inside, then led them to the reception desk, from where they ascended to the seventh floor, to the room reserved for them as a wedding gift. They entered the room hand in hand and walked around in it together, turned on the television, peeked into the shower and surveyed the row of miniature bottles and boxes and tubes that were arranged on the glass shelf below the mirror: liquid soap, shampoo, mouthwash, body lotion, a shower cap, a sponge to shine your shoes, a sewing kit, a shoehorn, a nail file.

They happily examined the bathrobes hanging on their hooks and the terrycloth slippers, opened the closet doors and noted the blankets and the iron and stood in wonder before the metal box that turned out to be a safe, opened the door of the small refrigerator and exclaimed at the abundance of drinks and candy it held, and went to the window to look out at the sea spread before them all the way to the horizon and the scantily dressed people walking along the promenade. And then Adella told Moshe to go and shower, and they released each other's hand. He was only there for a short time and emerged wearing the hotel bathrobe. Overcome at the sight, Adella went straight into the bathroom, hesitated for a moment and then turned the key. Inside the locked room she dumped the contents of all the little bottles into the bathtub and sank into a mountain of foam with a pleasure she had never experienced, ruining her fancy new hairdo in the process. That—Adella said now—was where her success began, with the decision she made while luxuriating in the bubbles that she would install a bathtub like that in her own home. But at the time she had no idea of the lengths to which her brothers- and sisters-in-law would go to prevent her from fulfilling her dreams.

When she came out she found Moshe fast asleep. She clearly recalled the instructions of the woman at the *mikve* from when she had immersed herself in the ritual bath before the wedding. The woman assigned to teach her about the laws of family purity had explained her obligations on her wedding night, and so she hesitated, not sure whether it was appropriate to wake him. These are things she has never divulged to a soul, but is willing to describe to me now, as I am already a married man and a father of twins, and she feels close enough to me to share these private details. She was indecisive, but he was in such a deep sleep, and she watched him for a while and in the end lay down beside him in the bed, and waited for him to wake up so that she could fulfil her duty, but he slept on, and she watched TV with the sound off, watched singers performing at a concert, and in the end she also fell asleep without turning off the television. They very rarely fulfilled the duties described by the woman at the *mikve*; Adella blushed and turned away, and I wondered why she chose to tell me this, for it was clear that she was also embarrassed.

In the morning she woke up before he did, Adella continues her story, relieved, as though the difficult part is behind her. She put on her glasses and looked over at his beautiful head on the pillow, reminding herself once again that yesterday she had married this man and he had put a ring on her finger. She watched him until he opened his eyes and asked if she had slept in her glasses and she answered that she had been awake for a long time. He jumped out of bed and handed her a box that his aunt had thrust into his hands after the wedding, which contained squares of cream cake and a stack of napkins. And so they sat and ate and wiped their mouths with the napkins, and each wiped traces of cream off the other's face and they laughed. They stayed in bed until the afternoon and watched a movie, unaware that they had missed the extravagant hotel breakfast. When they felt hungry they ate all the candy in the small refrigerator and went back to bed where they talked and kissed and told each other, "I love you," imitating the characters they had seen in movies. Several months before, after the wedding had been decided upon, they would part with a kiss on the cheek. Even under the wedding canopy, when they were a married couple, they kissed each other on the cheek. Now she laughed, describing their first kiss. She took off her glasses and leaned toward him, touched her lips to his, and closed her eyes, waiting for the new sensation. And they remained like that for a long time, not moving, making friends with this new feeling of lips touching lips.

Does it make me uncomfortable, this description? She glances sideways at me, she imagines that it doesn't. She assumes that I had this experience in my youth and not as a grown man of Uncle Moshe's age, who at the time was almost forty—she pauses for a moment, does the math—the same age that I am now. And that—now she looks me straight in the eye—is all they did on their honeymoon.

I want, but don't dare, to ask her why she is revealing these intimate memories, wondering and worried about just how far she intends to go. Most of my clients have shared more explicit stories, but she's talking about my Uncle Moshe, and I feel awkward.

"So how, how is all that connected to this store?" I try to move away from Adella's and Moshe's bed.

"It's connected to the sweater," she says now, referring to the colorful garment she showed me before the wedding, wrapped in silk fabric. On their second day in the hotel, the day when they were supposed to go home, Adella decided to show her husband the sweater, as a kind of test: if he liked it, that would be a good omen for the future, a sign from her mother. Not everyone liked that sweater: some thought it was too colorful, too vulgar. Carefully she slid it from the silk pouch she had sewn specially to protect it and arranged it, arms splayed, on the white bedspread, waiting for her husband's verdict. While he looked at the sweater she observed his face.

His expression of wonder at the beauty of what he beheld told her everything she needed to know, and they stood on either side of the sweater and gazed with love at the velvet fringes that dangled from the collar; the crocheted braids woven in several textures of colorful wool; the sleeves which from shoulder to elbow were studded with silk turquoise butterflies and the glittering stones dotting the sweater's hem. He whispered that it was a sweater fit for a queen and asked her to wear it for him, and to be a worthy companion to her elegance, he proposed that he put on his wedding suit again.

A short time later they emerged hand in hand into the hotel's large lobby and approached the coffee shop where breakfast was served. A friendly waiter noticed them standing lost at the entrance and approached them, asked for their room number, explained how the food was laid out, showed them to a table he chose for them and placed a carafe of coffee among the pretty dishes, with napkins folded into fabric swans floating upon them, next to a small glass vase holding one red rose. Their breakfast went on for a long time. Adella insisted on sampling every cake and every cookie and amused Moshe by closing her eyes and guessing at their ingredients: cinnamon and vanilla, regular flour mixed with semolina flour, too many eggs or not enough sugar.

After the meal, full to bursting, they held hands as they examined the display windows of the splendid stores, staring in amazement at the prices of a leather bag or a pair of men's shoes. As they lingered at the window of a women's clothing store the owner came out and approached them.

Adella hurried to explain, before she was accused of anything, that she was just looking and had no intention of buying anything, and the woman mollified her with a pleasant smile and said that they didn't have to make a purchase, she just wanted to ask where Adella bought her sweater. Still worried that she was about to be blamed for something, Adella said defensively that she had made it herself. The woman examined the sweater closely from where she was standing and asked Adella if she was sure that she hadn't bought it. Indignant now, Adella protested and repeated her declaration that she had made it with her own two hands, and Moshe came to her defense and repeated, "Her own two hands." To which Adella responded with a grateful squeeze. Not taking her eyes off the sweater, the store owner asked if she had knitted and crocheted all the elements herself and if she had chosen the beads, and Adella insisted that it was entirely her handiwork. And the woman said that in her opinion it was a very beautiful sweater, and she had customers who would grab it in an instant, and Adella's heart swelled inside her sweater.

On the bus, on the way home, Moshe thrilled at the memory of the encounter with the store owner. Adella smiled happily, and he kissed her on the cheek. Since they were feeling so relaxed and comfortable, she went ahead and spoke about what had been on the tip of her tongue for months, but she hadn't felt she could mention before the wedding, and then after the wedding she hadn't wanted to spoil the sweetness of the honeymoon with questions about money. Now, sitting practically alone on the big bus, out of earshot of the driver and the two passengers in the front seats, who were listening to a report on the radio about the celebrations planned for the arrival of Prisoner of Zion Natan Sharanksy, Adella felt it was the right moment and wondered aloud if she could ask some questions, explaining that they had to do with money. He looked surprised, as though he had suddenly plummeted to the ground from the luxurious room at the hotel. With bowed head he listened to her questions as though he was being pelted with stones: What would they live on, and how would they manage their income and expenses from now on? She herself, she hurried to reveal her own private affairs, had a bank account in her name, and she had managed to save 4,850 shekels from her salary at the lawyer's office. She suggested that they open a joint account and manage it together. How much money was in his account? How much did he earn each month? Lily had mentioned that he received disability benefits from the National Insurance Institute, so how much did that come to? And his father: she had been told that he would continue to live with them, who would cover his expenses?

For the first time since they met, Adella heard Moshe raise his voice and shout, "What expenses?" and he asked just what expenses the old man had.

And she quietly informed him that he ate, he drank, he showered, used soap and water, brushed his teeth; his sheets and towels and clothes needed to be washed, he used electricity, took medication, sometimes needed new clothes and shoes and socks—and while she spoke Moshe looked down, and his face shut down. In time, she smiles at me now, she learned what caused him to distance himself and erect a barrier between them, but that was the first time, and she didn't know yet that she had to leave him alone at moments like those, because when he withdrew into himself he didn't hear a thing. She kept on asking questions and pestering him until she understood. He had no idea whether he even had his own bank account. His siblings had managed his affairs all his life. They always saw to his needs and his father's needs too, and he had no clue how much he received in disability payments or how much they paid him for working at their stores.

Neither spoke on the walk home from the bus stop, each of them pulling along a suitcase. When they arrived the apartment was empty, and Moshe turned pale with fright, only calming down when his sister Vika explained over the phone that their father had taken ill and the doctor's orders were that he should stay with Lily until he was well enough to come back home. Adella stood close to him to hear whether she would ask about the honeymoon, but it seemed that Vika suspected that Adella was nearby, and all she said was that she hoped they had had a nice time, wished them both a pleasant evening and reminded him that the next day, Friday, he had to be at his brother Menashe's store at six o'clock in the morning.

They unpacked their cases in silence, separating the clothes to be washed from the items that would go into the closets. She made room for her things on some of the shelves. After that they sat at the table in the kitchen to eat a supper she prepared from food she found in the refrigerator and in the cupboards. She looked at Moshe and saw that he was on the verge of tears. She thought that the questions she had asked had forced him to confront the humiliating reality of his life because he was so distressed that he couldn't eat a thing. She tried to soothe him and told him in a soft voice that now that he had a wife he could manage his own affairs. She suggested that he ask his siblings to open a bank account for him if it turned out that he didn't have one, that they add her name and her savings and transfer his and his father's National Insurance payments to the account. From now on they would manage the account themselves, and in that way they would know how much they earned and how much they spent and how much they could save. He turned his back on her, pretending to look at the herbs in their pots along the windowsill, and didn't say a word. And then she surprised him and herself and asked if he loved her. He raised bewildered eyes from the plants, and when he realized that she was really waiting for his answer, he considered her question and replied that for the two days at the hotel he had thought that he loved her but ever since they boarded the bus he had felt confused by her. And she declared—and once again she surprised them both—that she loved him, and hadn't meant to confuse him.

He pondered her response and asked her if she truly loved him, and she immediately confirmed that she did. He was pleased with her reply, and as though testing her declaration he made a request: that she wouldn't speak to his siblings about the bank. She asked whether she would ever be able to raise the issue with them, or if for their entire lives they wouldn't be able to manage their own accounts themselves, and he requested six months. She asked why six months, and he explained that by then everyone would be used to her, positioning himself and his siblings as a united front. And she agreed. He was so happy about the reprieve that he went over to hug her, and the unpleasantness that had settled between them dissipated at once.

At the close of that evening—at this point Adella hesitates as if uncertain how much detail to reveal to me about that night, then takes a deep breath as if she has no choice but to forge ahead, and continues—after they ate and watched a comedy show on TV, they found themselves in the dusky shadows of the bedroom. Without exchanging a word, they separated the two single beds which were pushed together to make a double, consciously defying the clear instructions they had received, undressed and donned pajamas with their backs to each other, climbed into their separate beds, and only then did they wish each other goodnight in calm and pleasant voices. Adella tested the mattress and noted that its quality was as fine as the one in the hotel, and far superior to her mattress at the boarding school and also to those at the rented apartments. She smiled at the wall: there were things that would still have to be dealt with, but the future looked rosy with a handsome man at her side who came over and embraced her of his own free will.

Three days later the old man returned, weak and feeble, wanting only to rest or to sleep. He didn't notice the new curtain Adella had hung in his window or the pictures she bought with her own money showing deer posed in a clearing, birds soaring above water and expanses of wildflowers.

Slowly their lives began to settle into a routine, she tells me. Accustomed to rising early since her days at the boarding school, Adella was the first to awake, tugging herself abruptly from sleep and sitting up in bed. For just a second she wondered where she was, before she turned toward Moshe, stretched out on his back in his bed, and took in his beautiful face in repose. She gathered up the clothes she had chosen before she went to sleep and tiptoed to the bathroom. The house was still silent when she returned washed and shampooed and gently, with tiny taps of her fingertips on his forehead, woke Moshe. Sometimes she would wake him by slipping, fully dressed, under his bed-clothes, and he would open his eyes and smile and remember that she was waiting for him to hold her, and they would lie for long minutes with their arms around each other. She would rest her head on his chest and listen to his steady heartbeat. Then they would separate slowly and he would get dressed and wake his father while she set the table for breakfast with the same care as when she had helped to prepare the long tables at the boarding school for holiday meals, and never forgot to add a swan napkin, which she had taught herself to fold after seeing one on their table at the hotel in Tel Aviv. And when the men arrived at the breakfast table they were greeted by an omelet and fresh salad and warm bread, and on a small plate there would be a selection of her home-baked cookies. The elderly man sat scowling, but she and Moshe ate with quiet happiness, not allowing his anger to impinge on their sweet serenity, as if they knew that he was dissembling. After breakfast Moshe went to one of his brothers' stores, where he didn't have a set task, and was often moved from one to the other, as needed. And before he left for the day they would embrace at the door, a ritual they had observed in a movie they saw which they reenacted with warmth and joy. Adella devoted the first few days to her new home. Before the wedding she had noticed the disorganized kitchen cupboards and the jumble in the bathroom cabinets, and now she was free to empty them and decide what to keep and what would go into the cardboard box from the greengrocer's, and although she always kept an eye out for hidden bank statements or household receipts, even after emptying every shelf and drawer, not a scrap of a document was to be found.

From his spot in front of the television the old man watched her in furtive glances, saw how diligently she worked, humming softly to herself. Sometimes, when his chin fell to his chest, she made quick shopping trips. She had to save the receipts to present to Yosef at their weekly meetings. Occasionally she tarried at the bulletin board displayed in the window of the local real-estate agent where people in the neighborhood posted jobs: housecleaners, baby minders, jobs for clerks, messengers. Once she started to copy the telephone number of a caterer into her notebook, until she suddenly thought it might be a competitor of her brother-in-law Menashe's, since he owned the bakery, and she put her pen away on the spot.

In the evening Moshe would come home, his weariness plain on his face, in his walk and in the trembling of his hands. He would find his father facing the television, staring at the performance of an orchestra. A warm meal was always simmering in pots on the stove, and Adella's face lit up when she saw him.

On Fridays, before Shabbat, one of the siblings would arrive to escort the old man and the young couple to synagogue. Adella went upstairs with her sister-in-law to the women's section from where she looked down at the men, mostly at Moshe who would search for her and when his eyes alighted upon her would wave with a tiny, almost imperceptible movement, like a sign in a secret language, and with eyes tightly closed and a fluttering heart she prayed fervently for better days.

From the synagogue the small family returned home to eat their Shabbat meal together. On the following evening the extended family gathered as usual, as the siblings and their children came to visit their patriarch. At first the wives brought their baked goods and sandwiches, but as time passed there were fewer and fewer of their plates on the table, until all that remained were Adella's cakes and quiches, more delicious by far than anyone else's.

And each Saturday Yosef and his wife stayed on after all the others had left, which I already knew from my mother's long-distance phone calls. The wife would stay with her father-in-law, while Yosef and Adella sat down at the table. Moshe, impatient and awkward, sometimes hovered nearby, and sometimes next to his father and sister-in-law. Yosef gathered up the week's receipts, examined each one and added them up, inquired about the need for one item or another, issued a reprimand for the high price of a cleaning product or the coffee, a welcome mat or plants purchased at the florist's, examined the bus tickets and asked who was riding the bus and what were the destinations. That's how he learned that once a week Adella travelled to the boarding school to meet the teachers and visit the Holocaust survivor who lived nearby. And Adella explained patiently that she had visited the old woman once a week as part of the volunteer program all schoolchildren participated in in ninth grade, and had continued to visit her even after the year was over. With no hesitation, sparing her not the slightest glance, Yosef decreed to a shocked Adella that, henceforth, the trip to Givat Ada would be financed from her savings.

The first time Yosef went through the receipts Adella sat hunched in her chair, struggling to keep her emotions in check and answered every question without once looking up. On subsequent Saturday evenings she began to look pleadingly into his eyes, while he disregarded her humiliation.

After receiving a report for each receipt, Yosef would pull a fat wad of bills out of his pocket, thumb through it, withdraw some notes adding up to several hundred shekels for household expenses and leave them on the table, kiss his father, and leave. And Adella would immediately lean toward Moshe's ear and count down, "Five more months . . . Another month . . . Two more weeks . . . Next week the six months I promised will be over."

But before the six months were up a question occurred to Adella, although there was no one she could consult. She longed for a child. And how would they ever have a child when for months her husband hadn't joined her in her bed to fulfil the instructions necessary to create a family? It was true that at their first meeting the doctor had hinted that Moshe had some defect in that area, but in the same breath he had said that when the time came they could easily treat the problem, and he had no doubt that, with God's help, when the time was ripe, they would have children. One morning Adella went to see the doctor, and he was prepared to start to deal with the issue and asked her to come back with Moshe; for this procedure it was necessary for the couple to come together. However, before she had even left the doctor's office she knew that they wouldn't come to see him before the matter of the bank account was settled.

The week that marked the end of the period of silence to which she had acquiesced, before Yosef started to go through the receipts, Adella asked him if she could have a checkbook and access to their account. Yosef gave her an icy stare and replied in an over-loud voice that in their family women didn't speak that way. And while he was talking his gaze wandered to Moshe, evaluating his reaction to the events unfolding at the table, but Moshe hung his head, and his face was hidden in shadow. Adella straightened up, as if to counteract Moshe's posture, and in a steady voice said that she had to know how much money there was in her husband's bank account so that she could calculate herself how much she could spend, and she added that she also had personal expenses that she covered with her own money, and now she also had to pay for the bus rides as Yosef had instructed, but since she had no income her savings were dwindling and she didn't want anyone other than herself or her husband to be involved in their private expenses.

Yosef paid no attention to her question, snatched the receipts from her hand and began to inspect them one by one, but Adella refused to be cowed and in an even tone informed him that she was waiting for an answer and asked that he not insult her or her husband by ignoring them. Yosef looked up and leaned toward her menacingly, while in a controlled voice he said that in any case he was at the bank every other day so it was no problem to help out. He looked pointedly at Moshe as he hissed, "In our family we like to help each other," and immediately added, "Only I manage the account, and no one else." But Adella, undeterred, speaking softly despite the emotions seething within her, told him that her husband was almost forty, and they could manage their accounts themselves, and in any case she had to know what their income was, exactly how much her husband was paid for his work, how much she received in exchange for caring for the old man and how much her husband and her father-in-law received in social and disability benefits.

Through gritted teeth, Yosef asked what her expenses were, an orphan from a boarding school who had been given a home by good people. What more did she want now? To know what the expenses and the income were? Fine, the expenses—city taxes, water, electricity and gas—were all more than the income, so now what did she have to say?

"I'll get a job," she answered quietly. She wanted to cover her expenses herself: she wasn't asking anyone else to pay for her.

At that moment, Yosef's wife and his father, both of whom were sitting at the other end of the room on the corner of the sofa, turned toward her, as if seeing the real Adella for the first time. It seemed as though she was revealed to herself for the first time as well, for she looked directly into Yosef's eyes and said in a loud voice, so that the old man could also hear, that the money that Yosef left her once a month was not enough. She used her own money when that money ran out. The food for the last week's Shabbat table alone had cost her 120 shekels. Once more, in a softer voice, she repeated that the next day she and Moshe had to see the bank statements.

At this point Yosef turned to his brother and told him that Adella was in fact accusing him of cheating his little brother, of cheating Moshe, and that now he understood that they had brought a snake into the house who wanted to make trouble between the siblings, and maybe they should send this snake right back to the boarding school where it came from. And while he talked, he swept up the pile of receipts, pulled several bills out of his pocket and tossed them onto the table, patted Moshe on the back, kissed his father on the cheek, motioned to his wife to join him, and left.

Underneath the table, Moshe clutched at his stomach. And Adella herself, confused and frightened by the war she had declared, went over to the old man and asked him how he could allow Yosef to treat Moshe as though he was feeble-minded. As he knew, a woman was supposed to respect her husband. And how could she respect him if his own family didn't respect him? The old man's face crumpled. Did he see the devastation that was descending on his family? Was he frightened of the civil war that this foreign woman was bringing into his quiet home? Did he regret the arrival of his new daughter-in-law? Was he concerned about the dignity of his youngest son? Was he aware of the humiliations his son suffered?

He turned away from his daughter-in-law, but he couldn't block his ears, and so he heard her say that if the expenses exceeded the income, they would reduce the expenses. She didn't want his children's money. She was only asking him to tell his firstborn son to allow her to manage a bank account for her and her husband. They weren't little children who needed someone to manage things for them. From the age of ten she had been taking care of herself, and she wasn't about to let others tell her what to do now.

And then she returned to the table, cleared away the dishes, washed them, and without saying another word she left the room.

Now Adella suddenly turns pale and stops talking, and I am amazed at the ease with which she is snatched from the velvet armchair in her luxurious store to my grandfather's house almost thirty years before. She asks for a short break. She's feeling dizzy, and she has to lie down quietly. She'll rest while I go up to my room and get organized, and I can come back in an hour.

The room she reserved for me is on the seventh floor. When I look down at the beach through my window I wonder if it's a coincidence that I'm on the seventh floor, or whether she specifically requested the room where she and my Uncle Moshe spent their honeymoon. I take out my phone, switch off airplane mode and call my wife, Francesca—I still think of her as my wife, even though for the past six months I have been living on my own in a studio apartment in Angeles Court—and ask her to tell our twin teenage daughters that I landed safely. The telephone calls, with her and with the girls, are more pleasant than when we meet face-to-face. It's morning there, and she must be busy at the high school where she teaches art. Or maybe she's driving the girls to school and has decided to punish me. She received the sudden news about my trip with anger, even though we're separated. I shower, think about Adella's bubble bath, practically feel her presence in the steamy space, and hurry to towel off and leave the bathroom.

An hour later, when I step out of the elevator on my way to the row of stores, a woman in the coffee shop waves at me, her arm aloft. Adella. She's wearing a different dress, in bright butterfly colors. She seems to have recovered and looks relaxed again. I sit down opposite her, and she mentions that this is the same table where she and my Uncle Moshe ate breakfast on their honeymoon. And she signals to the waiter, as she lifts her small pot of coffee, to bring another one for me.

There are sometimes moments like that she confesses in a whisper, her eyes lowered to her coffee cup, when the past suddenly prevails, and then she is weak again, like the old Adella. It mostly happens if she wakes up when she's been dreaming. Dreams don't distinguish between past and present. Or sometimes someone comes into the store whose expression or voice or gestures remind her of a figure from the past. The more years go by, the more the past is poised to ambush her as the gap between it and the present widens. Now where, where was she? What was she talking about when she was suddenly overcome with fatigue?

"You were talking about the evening when you told my Uncle Yosef that you wanted to manage your husband's bank account."

Right, right. He didn't agree; she was immediately transported back to that moment: he insulted her and called her "the girl from the boarding school." After he left she had some tough words with her father-in-law. The next day Lily showed up at her father's house. It seemed that she had been sent to break the impasse, since she was the one deemed responsible for the rebellious bride who threatened to pollute the pleasant family atmosphere. Lily walked in without knocking, using her own key, and Adella watched as she snooped around. The house was tidy, the floor shone, and there was a fresh clean smell in the air; the old man was sitting in his armchair with a glass of tea and a plate of cookies by his side, and Adella was tending to the herbs on the windowsill in the kitchen. With honeyed words, Lily tried to convince Adella to drop the subject of the bank. But Adella insisted that Moshe and his father received payments from the National Insurance Institute, and she had to know how much they came to, how much Moshe earned at work, how much she was owed and what their living expenses were.

Lily stared at the girl in amazement, as though before her eyes she had been transformed into a different person. She told Adella that it was she, Lily, who was being held accountable for bringing Adella into the family and warned her that if she kept this up, things would end very badly. Before she left she said, "Remember, little people shouldn't pick fights with big ones." To which Adella replied in a level voice that she wasn't interested in a fight but in justice and went back to trimming the plants, concealing from Lily her shaking hands.

During the following days Adella barely spoke. At night she would get into bed without looking at Moshe. In the morning she put minimal effort into setting the table and didn't sit down to eat with Moshe and his father. If she noticed the old man slumped in his chair staring at a blank screen, unlike in the past she didn't change the channel for him. She made short work of the household chores and spent most of her time silently and feverishly knitting a new sweater. Moshe would look at her questioningly without saying a word. The old man, who by now was aware of her virtues and how much he depended on her, exchanged his customary scowl for an expression of bewilderment, as he tried to decipher her stony face. On Shabbat she didn't accompany them to synagogue, and on Saturday night when the family gathered there were no bottles of different kinds of drinks on the table, no homemade quiches or cookies or desserts, but water and salty snacks that she bought in bulk at the market.

It took her six days to knit the sweater, and she wrapped it lovingly, left the old man sleeping in his bed, took the bus to the hotel where she and Moshe had spent their honeymoon, swept through the revolving door, strode to the third store in the row of shops and presented the sweater to the owner of the boutique. She was happy to see Adella and exclaimed with delight over the sweater, turned it this way and that on the counter, stroked the velvet ribbons and the semiprecious stones, but was unsure of how to price a garment the likes of which she had never sold before. An elegant French tourist walked into the store and asked how much the sweater cost, and the flustered store owner told her that it wasn't for sale yet. After the woman left, she asked Adella how much she paid for her materials, and they agreed that they would split the profit. All the way home Adella calculated the number of hours she had spent working on the sweater and couldn't decide whether the deal she had made was worthwhile, but she kept recalling the radiant smile on the store owner's face when the sweater emerged from its wrapping.

On the day of the next weekly meeting to check the receipts, Yosef came early, arriving during the morning accompanied by his brother Menashe, as though bringing along a witness, and for the first time he asked Adella how she was. She immediately understood the significance of the visit for them, based on the unusual time of day and the fact that they had both absented themselves from their stores at such a busy hour. "Bad," she replied, and remained standing, facing the three seated brothers, as if refusing to participate in the meeting before her suspicions were allayed as to the nature of the visit. Yosef started talking right away and told her that on the following day the women would bring food to help her out. Adella didn't soften one bit and immediately retorted that they shouldn't do her any favors. That they weren't helping her, but themselves: the food was for them and for their families, and from the corner of her eye she observed the panic on Moshe's face.

Silence greeted her words, delivered in a loud, clear voice. For an instant it seemed as though Yosef's hand was about to rise to strike her. That the frail body of the young girl wouldn't withstand the blow and she would collapse, and who could tell what demons would be released from Moshe's trembling hands.

But none of these things happened. Yosef didn't raise his hand but rested it lightly on the table as he said: "My brother and I are ready to hear what you have to say. We don't want a war in our father's house."

She sat down. It seemed as though she was signifying her acquiescence by doing so, but it was her legs which reacted to the magnitude of the tension and gave out. This was not apparent in her voice, as she repeated her demand to be granted the responsibility to manage a joint bank account to belong to her and to Moshe, to ensure that the benefits that her husband and his father received from the National Insurance Institute were deposited into that account, as well as Moshe's salary for his work at his brothers' stores. "Work?" Menashe interrupted. Moshe didn't work for them. He came to the stores so he wouldn't sit around doing nothing at home.

A thud was suddenly heard as Moshe struggled to his feet and plummeted to the floor. From his spot in his wheelchair the old man gazed in horror at his sons, and a scream rose in his throat, like a warning of impending disaster. Adella hurried to Moshe, while the two sons rushed to their father. A short time later calm had been restored. Moshe had recovered and left for work with his brothers, and the father had taken his medicine and was sleeping peacefully in his bed.

But underneath the daily routines a growing unease was steadily brewing, which was evident in the powerful trembling that had revisited Moshe's hands and his father's frightened stare. The Saturday-night gatherings dwindled to visits from one sibling and his or her family at a time, as they took turns. Mostly they sat with the old man and watched television, barely relating to Moshe and ignoring Adella as if she didn't exist. She stopped setting out food and drinks for them and stayed in the bedroom, laboring over a new sweater.

Not long afterward the old man stumbled at synagogue and was taken to the hospital, where he died three days later.

For the entire week of the *shivah* mourning period, which was observed in the house where the old man had lived for most of his life, Adella stared repeatedly at my mother Michal, yearning for acknowledgement with either a nod or a greeting, hoping that she would approach her. Yes, yes—she looks straight at me now—she had been in sore need of a compassionate glance. But you didn't come, she scolds me now.

"My mother said that a boy who hadn't had his bar mitzvah yet isn't supposed to sit with mourners."

That was a shame, because there wasn't a single soul among all the people who crowded into the house who was sympathetic to her. All the siblings, even kindhearted Esther, simply behaved as if she didn't exist. Sometimes Moshe would find her crying in the bedroom, but he was consumed by his grief and the stomach pains that assailed him, and maybe he too, like his siblings, thought that it was she who had brought about the old man's death.

"And what happened after the *shivah*?"

Almost immediately after the *shivah* her period of slavery commenced. Four years of hell. Her eyes widen and glisten as images from that period appear unbidden, and she shakes herself, jumps to her feet, and says that she would prefer to stop talking.

"But we just got started . . ."

She didn't realize how much the conversation would exhaust her. Soon she has to close the store. It seems that she has talked enough for one day. And we still have three days left. Do I like to go to bars? There are excellent bars along this street and inside the hotel as well. The clerks at the reception desk can give me advice.

She strokes the entire length of my arm as she passes behind me on her way out and I realize that this is her parting gesture for the day.

"When should we meet tomorrow?"

She'll let me know. In any case, not before ten. I can eat dinner at the restaurant at the hotel and charge it to the room, and I should feel free to take as much as I want from the mini bar—she's already walking away without another word of farewell, and I watch as she hurries toward the store, fending off the memories by escaping into her fortress. As I follow her with my eyes I see what I hadn't noticed before: the energetic walk, her pelvis propelling her briskly forward, the arms churning while held close to her sides, and yet there is still something that perhaps only I can discern, the faint shadow of a limp.

Neither of us has referred to my bar mitzvah celebration. My father didn't turn up, and my ill Uncle Moshe dragged himself to the synagogue and then returned straight to his bed, leaning on Adella, whose downcast eyes never left the floor.

I finish my coffee and go down to walk along the beach, trying to organize my thoughts, but her stories, my memories, and the fragments of information that reached me in Los Angeles seem to be at odds. Usually by this time I can already draft an outline for the structure of the story, the first version of the chapter headings, but this time, unlike all the others, I decide to wait until the following day, when things may become clearer and perhaps I will understand why I was asked to come. In the meantime I walk barefoot on the sand, drawn backward in time to the fifteen-year-old self I left behind, but the boy who departed has changed so much from the one who remained that I have no way of piecing the two together. People walk by, speaking to one another in Hebrew interspersed with words I have never heard before. Enveloped in a strange fog of belonging and estrangement I take out my phone, which is still in silent mode. The display is crammed with missed calls, four of them from my wife. Did she call to tell me that she has found a new man and wants to speed up the divorce, or does she want me to know that the twins are missing me, and she is too?

She doesn't answer, and I am filled with unease. It must have been something urgent if she tried to reach me four times. Has something happened to the twins? Has there been an accident? For the next three hours as I keep trying her number and she never picks up I tell myself that she may have left her phone in one of the classrooms, or it might have been stolen at the mall downtown where she takes the twins for pizza, or maybe she muted it in one of her classes and forgot about it. I send a text: "Is everything okay?" and then, "I couldn't answer." And a few hours later, "I'm going to sleep, but I'm leaving the phone next to me, call me."

And when I fall asleep on the white sheets my last thought isn't about my estranged wife or the twins but, to my surprise, about Adella and Uncle Moshe's bridal bed.

In the morning there's a brief message waiting for me on the phone's display, angry, but not totally hostile: "How could everything be okay? How are things with you?" As if I hadn't tried to reach them for three straight hours before I fell asleep. I subdue my anger and send an emoji of a man doing exercises: "I guess nothing terrible happened. Why did you call? I tried to reach you . . . By the way, the hotel is fine. I'm still not sure whether this is a work trip or a visit. When can I talk to the girls?" My questions go unanswered.

When I walk into the store at ten, Adella rushes over to me as though she is in grave danger and has finally spotted some- one who can rescue her. I look at her and immediately see that her eyes are different from the eyes I looked into the day before, as though she hasn't slept a wink or has been up the whole night crying.

"We won't sit here in the store today." She swipes a bunch of keys from the hook hanging over the counter. "Naama will come soon, and until then the store can stay closed, it's no big deal." She flips over the "Be Right Back" sign and locks the door. "And we won't sit in the hotel coffee shop either: my cli- ents may disturb us there when they find the store closed. We'll go to the café across the street, we can hide out there." She's already approaching the revolving doors, and I'm right behind her.

Inside the café she settles into a wicker chair and takes off her sunglasses. I study her: eyes exposed and alert, pleasant face, limber body. Adella has come a long way with her transformation into Adel. She asks if I slept well, if I enjoyed my breakfast. And then she declares that this morning we will talk about me. She's so curious to know what I've been doing for the past twenty-four years, what it was like when I first arrived in Los Angeles. I was very sick when I was at her house, and my mother took me away against the doctor's wishes. Yes, yes, the doctor was really opposed, didn't my mother tell me? She told me that the doctor agreed? It wasn't the same doctor who had taken care of me when I was sick. The doctor who agreed that I could travel—if he was even a real doctor—was someone my mother found, God knows where. After two weeks during which the two of them took care of me together they had reconciled, but they parted in anger again because of the permission granted by the fake doctor and my mother's insistence that she be the only one to look after me. Adella thought that I needed more time to recover, and even suggested that my mother return to Los Angeles if she had to and that she, Adella, would accompany me on the plane once I was better. But my mother was like someone possessed at that time. She argued with everyone, lost control, declared that she was the only one permitted to enter my room. So how, how was the flight in the end? She had worried constantly until she heard that I landed safely.

"I slept for most of the flight, I don't remember anything. I only remember that my father and my brother and sister met us at the airport."

And when I arrived in Los Angeles, was I still sick? Did I have any memory of my illness?

"I slept for three solid days and then we all went out, the

whole family, to a restaurant. And soon after that my father started looking for a school for me."

And . . . and did I remember the period when I was sick at her house? They were all very frightened. The doctor was so concerned. What . . . Did I remember anything from that time?

"I remember the exam. I started to feel bad in the middle of it. I remember they brought me a bottle of water. I remember the gym teacher's car. I don't remember giving her your address, but I must have because she brought me to your house. And after that I don't remember anything until they put me in a wheelchair and took me to the airport. When we got to the escalator I stood up and my uncles took the chair."

She interrogates me with a piercing stare. Caught in a shaft of sunlight her eyes shine like glass. And how, she wonders, choosing her words, how did we find out . . . that she was pregnant with Elisha?

"That was when my mother was still talking to everyone. We got an update every Friday night, at dinner. On one of those Fridays my mother told us that you were pregnant."

And so, what did we think? What did my mother say? What did I think?

"Everyone was happy for Uncle Moshe."

And me, what did I think?

"I was also happy for Uncle Moshe. And also for you." The lie slides out smooth as silk.

Her eyes scour my face for another moment, scrutinizing me.

"Very good," she says, and it's clear that all at once she has lost interest. Tonelessly she enquires about my brother, my sister, and my father, and the warmth only returns to her voice when she asks how my mother is doing. She listens somber-faced to my descriptions of the visits to the home, shaking her head sorrowfully when I describe the last time I saw my mother and our parting only four days before, and encourages me to keep on visiting her. And as if to somehow counter the empty life that has been my mother's lot for the past twenty years, she once again mentions the selfless battle my mother fought for her after her first visit to my grandfather's house.

I expect her to be more curious about the woman I married, to ask how we met, when we started dating, why I chose to marry her, what kind of wedding we had, when she became pregnant, how the birth was, when we found out we were having twins. How the twins developed. But she doesn't say a word, as if she's still thinking about my mother, and I understand that her interest in me is limited to the boy I was when she knew me.

Since that is the case, I ask her a question designed to bring us back to the point where we left off the day before.

"How was it, the time you call your 'period of slavery'?"

She pales, retreats further into her silence, takes a deep, quavering breath and begins to whisper a description of those years. Right after the *shivah* for their father, even before they erected the tombstone, Yosef informed her, as the family representative, that the apartment had been inherited by all the siblings together. Up until then Moshe had lived at his parents' house for free, but now he would have to pay rent, minus one-eighth, which was his portion of the inheritance. Yosef regarded Adella over Moshe's head as he spoke to him, as if declaring that this was all her fault and his younger brother was suffering because of her. She wanted the bank account? Fine. Now she didn't have to look after her father-in-law so she also wouldn't get his benefits. She would see for herself that the disability payment her husband received from the National Insurance Institute wouldn't even cover bread and cheese. She wanted him to be paid for his work? Fine. But from now on they wouldn't be receiving the weekly allowance. She would have to provide for them from the money in the account.

At the conclusion of the mourning period for his father Moshe's pains worsened, and nothing the doctors suggested provided him with any relief, so that Adella had no choice but to work in his place to cover the rent and their living expenses. For four years, minus the short periods when Moshe did his best to go back to work, each and every one of his siblings abused her, punishing her for daring to demand her independence, for insulting the men, for the bad example she set for the women, for the family that fell apart because of her, for the deterioration in their father's condition. She was forced to rise early to help prepare the challah at Menashe's bakery, and on Fridays she worked right up until Shabbat, just before the sun set. They didn't give her a moment's rest, sent her to clean the toilets in the stores and laughed about her behind her back, but always within earshot—about the bathtub she asked to have installed instead of the shower, about the eye surgery she wanted to undergo, about the special shoes she wanted to order to disguise her limp. She tries to repress the memories of those four years, because they awaken a desire for revenge. She prefers to concentrate on positive feelings and to look back in wonder at herself, at how she didn't sink into despair over the trap she had been forced into, at how she cared for Uncle Moshe, at how she continued to knit her sweaters for all those years and even taught Moshe how to knit. It's true that he wasn't able to work, but he would travel to the store at the hotel to deliver the results of their monthly labors and to deposit what they earned into their joint bank account.

"And how did you ever manage to escape the trap?"

"It's all thanks to you." Her eyes shine.

"To me?" I say the words, not understanding what part I could have played in her life at that time.

"Yes, yes." She gazes into my eyes, amused by the confused expression on my face. Her destiny was reversed the moment I arrived, collapsing with fever, on her doorstep. And when she opened the door, she was also opening it to her good fortune, and the two of us, me and her good fortune, walked into the house together. Right after I left for Los Angeles with my mother she was blessed with her pregnancy. From the moment she presented Yosef with the results of the pregnancy test and the doctor's letter saying that hers was a high-risk pregnancy which necessitated bedrest, her period of enslavement came to an end. She left the stores, never to return. Moshe helped out when his health allowed it, and Adella would keep a record of his hours, calculate how much he had earned based on a booklet published by the Labor Federation and ensure that the precise sum was transferred to their bank account. She spent most of each day sitting in her bed, protecting the precious fetus that slowly developed, delighted to see that she was turning out particularly spectacular sweaters. Occasionally one of the girls from the boarding school would be sent over to spend a Shabbat with her to help with the housework that Adella couldn't ask Moshe to tend to. At sundown Moshe would go on his own to the family gatherings, which after the death of the old man rotated from house to house each week.

And then Elisha was born. In a difficult, drawn-out labor which endangered his mother's life for a full twenty-four hours; but once the danger had passed there was no end to their joy. The celebration for his circumcision, the *brit milah* ceremony, was held at their home, and once again it brought all the siblings together, including the couple from Jerusalem who attended without their children, to share in their youngest brother's sudden joy. But even this happy event didn't merit Adella more than one or two limp handshakes, as if to make it clear that they had no doubts that this pregnancy and birth were nothing but a ruse, so she could sneak out of working at the stores.

Adella spent the entire first year of his life, until he was weaned, with Elisha. That was also when she found a specialist shoemaker and ordered shoes that allowed her to walk smoothly. Now she has shoes like those in different colors, but back then she had only one brown pair. Once a week she would go to the boarding school to visit the teachers and Mrs. Berta who gave her the suitcase of fabrics. Did I remember that suitcase? Yes, yes, she thought that I would. It had belonged to the Holocaust survivor. She had labored over its contents at the school for seamstresses before the war, and a kind Polish neighbor had kept the suitcase safe for her. After the war she collected it and went to live in Israel, and when her husband died she supported her two sons with her sewing. Every time Adella came to visit they would knit together and Mrs. Berta would show her the notebooks, and because Adella was so interested in the fabrics, Mrs. Berta decided to give her the suitcase as a gift, knowing that she would take care of it, whereas a time would come when her sons would surely toss it on the trash heap.

On the day when she went to visit Mrs. Berta and the teachers Adella would leave Elisha in Moshe's care, setting out early in the morning and returning in the evening exhausted but overflowing with enthusiasm and plans and sketches. She convinced the principal to set up a sewing department at the boarding school. And a month later Mrs. Berta said that she would donate a sewing machine and a knitting machine. And two weeks later, despite the fact that she was nearing eighty, she announced that once a week she would come to the boarding school to teach the girls how to sew. The principal, who was eager to put the plan into action and had even located a suitable teacher to manage the department, had to wait for approval from the office in Jerusalem, which took a long time to arrive. And in the meantime Adella did her best to garner the support of the girls, enticing them with a display of her own creations. During the same period, the small bakery at the school, where Adella had learned to prepare cookies and quiches, was expanding. Two new ovens and a large blender were donated by an electric appliance store so that production increased considerably. Next to the gate there was a small empty room once used as a waiting room for guests. With a small investment the space was transformed into a shop where the baked goods were sold. When Adella told Moshe about it, and expressed concerns about whether the new shop would be a success, he advised her to devote prayers to the matter.

On fine days Adella would push the stroller to a new bustling commercial center, and with time on her hands she would wander at her leisure and gaze at the store windows, a pleasure that had been an unattainable fantasy during the four years that preceded her pregnancy. And that's how one day she found herself at a real-estate office. From the advertisements for apartments for sale or for rent that were posted in the window she learned that she and Moshe were paying an inflated price for their apartment, which was situated on the ground floor squashed between the pillars that supported the building, with the only natural light coming through the window in the kitchen for a few short hours each day, just enough to allow the herbs to flourish in their pots along the windowsill. Among the ads for apartments offered for sale she saw new, brightly lit apartments with plenty of kitchen cabinets which cost double the amount that they had accumulated in their bank account.

At the end of the row of shops was a lawyer's office. Adella peeked inside and thought she saw a boy sitting there. She asked him where his father was and was most embarrassed when it turned out that he was the lawyer. Even though he was clearly accustomed to such questions and wasn't the least bit upset, the blush didn't fade from her cheeks until they had concluded their long meeting.

In that office, she tells me now with a smile, she found a true friend. The two individuals with their respective defects immediately formed an alliance. He asked her to sit down, and with Elisha on her lap she told the lawyer some of the details about the conditions of her life in the apartment that was an inheritance. And it seemed that he also understood the parts that she left out. He asked for details about their savings and regular income, and she listed the disability payment and the steady income from the sweaters and added an average for the fluctuating amount that Moshe earned working for his brothers. Then he described various options, such as buying a small apartment of their own or purchasing a larger one with a mortgage, or buying a larger one for key money without a mortgage, and explained the differences and the advantages and disadvantages of each of the possibilities, and promised to help her to make the best choice and to ensure that a bank clerk he knew would approve a loan so they could come up with the required amount.

Her head bursting with possibilities for a new life, Adella told Moshe all about her day and showed him the photographs of the new apartments, to which he responded with an expression of abject terror. Stammering, he told her that he was sure that this new apartment would come between him and his siblings. Greatly dismayed, Adella replied that his caring brothers and sisters would be happy to see him in a well-lit apartment and tried to convince him that she and Elisha were his family now, and that they should come before his siblings. And again she showed him the photographs of the apartments, in one of which there was a beautiful, gleaming bathtub. When night fell, after she had bathed Elisha and nursed him and put him to sleep in his bed, she sat with Moshe and persuaded him that Elisha deserved a nice room with light and sunshine and a big window, like the room that had belonged to Yarden where they had met by themselves for the first time. At the memory of that meeting they both smiled and embraced. And then Moshe asked that she not raise the subject of the new apartment again for six months, and she agreed.

The next time she went to the commercial center, when she walked past the window of the real-estate office she turned away from the pictures of the apartments, but her eye was caught by the word "stores," and she saw square notices offering stores for rent. Moving closer to the window, focusing on the two rows of notices about stores, she discovered that one of them was on the same street as the stores owned by her brothers-in-law. In no time she and Elisha were squashed in the backseat of the realtor's car, which soon stopped at an address at the top of the street, within sight of the clothing store and the bakery she knew so well.

The store itself, formerly the office of a taxi company, was quite pleasant. A large window at the front faced the street, and an even larger window faced the backyard where there was a bench and a straw mat spread on the ground. In her mind's eye Adella immediately saw where the shelves with their trays of bread should stand, where the boxes of cookies should be placed, where the coffee corner would be, the counter where the cash register could sit, and how the remaining space would be perfect for two small tables by the window looking out onto the street. Near the entrance there was a staircase that led to an upper floor with a low ceiling that currently housed two sofas and a bathroom with a broken door. She asked the realtor to photograph the place from every angle and on the spot made the decision not to tell Moshe about it, for he would certainly be frightened about potential competition with his brother Menashe's bakery, where he still occasionally worked.

The next day, Adella picked up the photographs and took them to the office of her friend the lawyer, who promised to put her in touch with a business consultant who would advise her about how to manage the store for several months after it opened.

Only then did Adella go to see the principal of the boarding school to show her the photographs and the evaluation she had requested from the business consultant as well as the entire business plan, which she had worked out to the last detail. She would manage the store herself, at first from morning to evening. Every two days the boarding school would send her a delivery of fresh baked goods that she would sell in bags stamped with the symbol of the school. Every Thursday after school two girls from the boarding school—according to a roster—could come to work at the store during what would be the busiest days until it closed on Friday afternoon. They would help to clean the store and before Shabbat fell they would make their way home or back to the school, or if they preferred they could stay with her for the weekend, on the sofa bed in Elisha's room. The principal took a long time to examine the photographs and the documents, trying to make up her mind. They both knew that the small shop in the room by the entrance had turned out to be a failure. Beautiful cakes and cookies remained on the shelves until they turned hard as rocks. The saleswoman spent many hours there on her own and no customers appeared. Soon they would have to empty it out, and it would return to its dreary origins. Adella confessed that she had anticipated the failure of the store because no one passed by except for employees and the rare guest. In contrast, the store in the photographs spread out in front of her was located on a main street, and hundreds, if not thousands, of people passed it every day. The uncertain principal noted that it was quite far from the school, and Adella didn't deny it, pointing out that any central location was far from the boarding school, and that this one was even a little farther away. However, if she, Adella, were to manage the store, it had to be close to her home because of the baby. And then the principal wondered aloud whether Adella had any experience managing this type of store, and Adella told her about the four years during which she had worked at a bakery and seen how it was managed, reminded her about the accountant and the business consultant who would be advising her, and added that the girls would gain experience, the expenses were low, and the chance of success was high, not to mention that the lawyer had promised to persuade the owner of the store to lower the rent because of the boarding school, and that the expenses could be further reduced if they brought the shelves and the baskets from the little room near the gate. Also, if the owner of the electrical appliance store agreed, they could transfer the ovens to the new store.

It took the principal two weeks to make up her mind. And even then she didn't say much, just pursed her lips. When Adella handed her the rental contract and the agreement written up by the lawyer about the division of expenses and profits among the parties to the agreement, she stared at the wording and said she had to get the approval of the boarding school's legal advisor. He rewrote several clauses, so that they now said exactly the same thing, but in different words.

The moment approval was given, Adella wondered about the best way to tell Moshe about the big change that was about to take place in their lives. She altered some of the plot details, presented the principal as the one responsible for the initiative, convinced Moshe that it was for a good cause, and reassured him that since it was on a different part of the street it wouldn't be competition for his brother. Despite the mournful look on his face, she informed him that for at least the first few months she would have to stay at the store until the evening, so that he would have to coordinate his work hours with the hours of the woman whom she had hired to take care of Elisha. He tried to protest, but her points were better marshalled and more persuasive; he became flustered, and in the end he gave in.

Two days after the renovations began Menashe appeared at the entrance to the store and was shocked to find Adella there, overseeing the labor of two workers who were unloading shelves, ovens, and a counter from a truck parked outside. I smiled a secret smile as I imagined the scene.

"They say there's going to be a bakery here." He peeked inside, unable to meet the eyes of the woman who not long before had meekly received his instructions and never dared to open her mouth.

"Wait and see," she replied in an ordinary voice, "In the meantime, you're in the way, these people are trying to work."

Thus rebuked, he stayed there a little longer, moving left and right as per the workers' requests, and finally rushing off to his brother Yosef's store.

Adella returned home that evening to find Moshe rocking Elisha to sleep, his face the picture of doom. Yosef had phoned him and warned that the store would be burned down within a month if it opened. Kneeling before him, Adella grasped his legs and told him that they both knew his brother: Yosef might make threats, but he wouldn't dare to act. So confused by the sight of his wife on her knees, Moshe blurted out the information he had so far withheld. His brothers had fired him, claiming that he was party to his wife's plot. To his surprise and amazement, his revelation delighted her. The woman she had hired to take care of Elisha was good at her job, she told him with shining eyes, but there was no better caregiver than a parent. He could take care of Elisha himself, and they would save money, and Adella could devote her attention to the new project without the slightest worry.

The following day Adella went to the police and lodged a complaint against Yosef. From there she continued to the realtor's office where she asked him to find an apartment for rent in the vicinity of the new store. Next, she visited the lawyer, where she asked him to draft three letters and send them to Yosef. The first was a warning to him to stop issuing threats, the second demanded the severance pay owed to Moshe now that his employment had been terminated, and the third informed him of their intention to vacate the grandfather's apartment, put it up for sale, and receive their share of the profits. She didn't show any of the letters to Moshe and concealed her own trembling hands inside her purse.

For two days—until the shock dissipated—not one of the siblings came near the new store, which was now being painted.

But on the third day Vika walked past slowly on the sidewalk and stopped at the entrance. The two women had last seen one another nearly a year before, at the celebration for Elisha's circumcision. Now Vika and Adella stood face to face like adversaries in the ring, sizing up the changes that had taken place in the other woman over the past months. Then Vika leaned deliberately into the doorway and spat her curse, only to be treated to the sight of a slow smile of victory spreading across Adella's face. Vika turned away, straightened her shoulders, and continued down the street.

On opening day, which was planned for a Thursday, one of the busiest shopping days of the week, six girls from the boarding school arrived. Smiling and excited, they filled the small store with youthful energy, and in pairs they took turns to stand on the sidewalk and offer laden trays to the passersby, urging them to sample the cookies and slices of fresh bread.

During the first month the store was open Adella learned which cookies sold well and which dried out in their baskets, which types of bread were the most popular and which were sent back to the boarding school. The business consultant came, spread his charts on the table and advised Adella to add a refrigerator for drinks and a coffee machine, and to start to pay the girls from the profits. Soon there were regulars at the shop, and Adella remembered what they liked and would win them over by including a free piece of cake or some cookies with their purchases. She was like a tender mother to the girls, but anyone who was sloppy or lazy or rude to the customers wasn't invited back to work. Sometimes Moshe would visit the store with Elisha, and during the peak hours he would leave the child in a playpen in the yard where they could see him through the window and pitch in. About Moshe—Adella hesitated now—she had to confess, his spirit was irrevocably broken after the split in relations with his family. He was aware of the fact that they had been deteriorating for years, but he sorely missed the weekly gatherings. On the holidays, although they never failed to invite some of the girls from the boarding school, and Elisha's laughter filled the house, she was always aware of the sadness in her husband's eyes.

The store was closed for a week over the Pesach holiday, and Adella realized her dream to have eye surgery. She locked the door wearing her usual thick-lensed glasses, and after the holiday she reopened for business with lightly made-up, sharply focused eyes, basking in the looks of astonishment on the faces of her customers, some of whom didn't even recognize her at first.

Occasionally, in quiet moments, she would walk over to the door, lean against the entrance and look out at the businesses that belonged to Menashe and Yosef, as if observing herself from another era. After the complaint was lodged with the police and the lawyer's letter had been dispatched, none of the siblings dared to come near the store again, and with pent-up rage they paid Moshe what they owed him. Soon after, the small family moved to a better-lit rented apartment owned by an elderly man. He was pleasant when they signed the contract but subsequently made their lives miserable, appearing in their home at odd hours and asserting that such surprise visits in no way contravened their agreement.

A year after the store opened, when the accountant displayed a balance sheet which showed healthy profits from the previous months, a joyful celebration was held in the principal's office at the boarding school to toast the success of the project, and all the girls who worked at the store were in attendance. When everyone had left and only Adella and the principal remained, the older woman embraced her and told her that upon the advice of the accountant she had agreed to double Adella's salary. Unaccustomed to such gestures of generosity, Adella promptly burst into tears.

And for all that time she and especially Moshe continued to turn out the sweaters that became more colorful and detailed as they discovered new treasures such as chiffon ribbons, silks, and decorative buttons. They set up a desk in their living room especially for the sweaters, and there was always a garment spread across its surface that they were working on. Its drawers were bursting with an assortment of materials and finished sweaters wrapped in delicate crepe paper.

"Is the store still there?"

"No, not anymore." For several years, until Elisha was older and didn't need round-the-clock supervision, the store Adella had created was frequented by a regular customer base that developed around it, and the boarding school enjoyed a tidy income. During that period it expanded and became a bustling café. When the adjacent shop, which sold building supplies, closed down, they rented it for a low price, broke through the adjoining wall and created the coffee shop. And when she was firmly established at the boutique at the hotel, Adella left the café, and it was managed by one of the graduates of the boarding school who had worked there for two years. Only when she was satisfied that the young woman could do the job well did Adella hand over to her. Not many years later the woman married and moved with her husband to the north of the country, and the principal, who was on the verge of retirement, decided to close the place.

"And what happened with the sweaters?" I didn't understand why I felt so flustered as I gestured toward the hotel across the street.

For the seven years when she ran the bakery and the café Adella and Moshe had continued to make sweaters to sell at the boutique. During that period, in addition to a business connection, a personal relationship was woven between them and the owner of the store, who was besotted with Elisha and showered him with gifts. Since Adella was motherless, and the woman's only daughter had followed her husband to Germany—he was a German man she had met at that very hotel when she was serving in the army—in addition to the commercial connection and the friendship they also shared something akin to a mother–daughter relationship.

Then came the attractive opportunity to replace the senior saleswoman, who was about to retire, and the offer of a generous salary in addition to Adella's profits from the sale of her sweaters. The owner had found herself travelling more frequently to visit her daughter in Germany, and in any case Adella often stopped by the boutique, bringing a sweater or two that she and Moshe had worked on together and a basket of baked goods, and each time she had learned something—from new management techniques to fashion and beauty tips. So for a while Adella managed both the café and the boutique, juggling her time, finding workers for one place, closing the other one earlier than usual, until she decided to concentrate on the boutique, to make changes there, and to apply what she had learned from her work at the café.

"And Grandfather's apartment?"

It just sat there and rotted. For years she and Uncle Moshe received their miniscule monthly share, which was routinely deposited late.

Then one day after a conversation with the lawyer, something occurred to Moshe and it took shape, and he convened all his siblings in Menashe's store after closing time and with great passion berated them for taking care of themselves, every one of them, and ensuring that they had a roof over their own heads, but never thinking to open a savings account for him so that he could buy an apartment someday, even though for all those years he had worked for them in their stores. They had misled him to believe that his parent's apartment was his home. It was the first time in his life that Moshe had dared to confront his astonished siblings, and before he had a chance to regret his courageous act, he withdrew a slip of paper from his pocket and read aloud what the lawyer had printed for him: "Dissolution of a partnership is discussed in accordance with section 37(a) of real estate law 5769. The section of the law grants each of the owners of a common real estate property the right to dissolve the partnership at any time. Joint ownership is a temporary and undesirable situation and its dissolution is a basic right of every partner so that the court almost never intervenes to prevent its execution."

The room was completely silent. Three sisters and two brothers turned to their baby brother, the disabled one, in shock. There was no hiding his trembling hand which gripped the piece of paper, but there was also no denying the determined tone of his steady voice as he read out the text prepared for him by the lawyer in legalese. They all understood. They had no choice but to sell their parents' apartment.

When the shock wore off there came a period of arguments among the siblings. Yosef claimed that at his parents' request he had invested his own money in the apartment, financed the addition of kitchen cabinets and replaced the windows and the shutters, and therefore he should have a larger share than the others; Vika said that she had cooked and cleaned at her mother's behest during the last year of her life and her daughters had slept over to take care of their grandmother, who had promised that in return Vika would receive a larger portion of the inheritance.

Adella learned of all this from her lawyer, who represented her in the matter and finally had no choice but to seek a court ruling which determined that the apartment had to be sold.

"So in the end Grandfather's apartment was sold?"

"Sold in the end, yes, your grandfather's apartment. The siblings screamed and yelled." Adella smiles at the happy memory. Yosef went out of his way to incite the others against her and Moshe, and found an unexpected ally in the brother in Jerusalem, who sent a delegation of the sisters to appeal to Moshe and remind him that more than anything else their parents had wanted their children to live in harmony. For a while their appeals seemed to be working. No, no. She didn't get involved. Sometimes wars happen of their own accord and they benefit you and you don't have to lift a finger. She left Moshe to it, torn between her and his siblings, and meanwhile continued the search for an apartment.

Around the time when they moved into the rented apartment the relationships with his siblings slowly petered out. This caused Moshe great sorrow, for he understood that they had renounced him, claiming that Adella had poisoned him against them. However, his awareness of their unjust behavior toward him and his love for Adella and Elisha softened the pain of the separation. Meanwhile, during all those years Adella worked as a saleswoman at the boutique, transformed their rented apartment into a warm home, supervised their savings and nurtured her dream to purchase a home of their own. She went to see old apartments that were for sale and to examine plans for new ones slated to be built.

One day, Adella brought plans for a new apartment block to work with her, and asked the owner for her opinion and advice, and the older woman was overcome at the coincidence and saw it as a good omen, for that same day she had intended to ask Adella if she would consider taking over the store for an extended period because her daughter in Germany was expecting a child and urging her mother to come and live with her for a while until the child started school. She had complete trust in Adella's integrity and loyalty she told her, and if she agreed to manage the store, her monthly income would increase and her extraordinary sweaters would have a permanent home. She added that she had even thought of a new name for the boutique—Adel.

The two women embraced, the one full of joy about a new grandchild, the other about the clothing store. And then the grandmother-to-be told Adella about an apartment on nearby

Ben Yehuda Street, which she knew was for sale because she had seen a sign affixed to the balcony advertising the fact.

Adella arrived at the apartment to find the door ajar and the movers carrying out the furniture. Standing at the entrance, even before she had set foot inside, she could see the sea rippling like a silk scarf beyond the balcony and was suffused with an elation she recalled experiencing at the hotel that was just one street over, on the first morning of her honeymoon. The next day she brought Moshe and placed the decision in his hands.

From that point—really from the moment when the door of the apartment opened to Moshe and he was greeted by that expanse of blue, walked to the balcony, and spread his arms as though to embrace the horizon—things moved quickly. At Adella's request the "For Sale" sign was immediately taken down. Their lawyer, who knew all the details about the money they had in the bank, came to an agreement with the lawyer who was handling the sale for the owners, an elderly, well-off couple who were moving to a retirement home. Adella and Moshe's lawyer managed to reduce the price, to organize a modest bank loan, and to draw up a satisfactory contract. Elisha was already nine years old.

"And that was it—once you moved there was no more contact with my aunts and uncles?" I asked sadly. And a minute later I thought: I'm sad for myself. The sentence I had uttered had pained me.

The connection was broken before, when Adella and Moshe requested that they sell their father's apartment, and gradually the siblings had stopped inviting them to family events. It was around the time when his wife became the manager of the clothing store that Moshe chose not to go to the synagogue that he had attended for most of his life, and with that he stopped seeing his brothers and sisters. That's when he started to create items that they hadn't thought of before. Scarves and wallets and belts in the style of the sweaters, and they sold them at the store as well. Any time his heart shifted in the direction of his relatives, he would remind himself about how unfairly they had treated him, each and every one of them, either directly or indirectly. And once he, Adella, and Elisha had moved from the rented apartment to their new home in Tel Aviv he never ran into any of his siblings in the street.

Years later she met one of the nephews on a Tel Aviv beach and learned that Vika had died of a heart attack. He listed who was married and who had children and who had celebrated a bar mitzvah. Moshe burst into tears when Adella relayed the conversation and was deeply unhappy for an entire week.

Some years after that, one of the nieces happened to walk into Adella's store, fall in love with an embroidered shirt and purchase it at a substantial discount. Adella invited her for coffee at the hotel coffee shop, as usual making for the table where she and Moshe had eaten breakfast on their honeymoon. And as they sat there the niece recounted who had died and who had married and who had given birth and who had moved and who was sick, and Adella never said a word about any of it to Moshe. A broken connection is permanent. "It's a knack this family has," she says now with a bitter smile, noting that my mother was also blessed with it.

"And don't you ever think about them?"

Once in a while, mostly when those Jewish holidays came around that we still celebrated in America, or on rare visits to the synagogue, I thought of them myself.

Mostly she feels angry, her face clouds. Moshe feels pain and she feels anger. Occasionally, she whispers now as if making a confession, on the way to the boarding school in Givat Ada her curiosity gets the better of her, and she asks Alex to make a detour and drive past my Uncle Yosef's and my Uncle Menashe's stores. Their sons manage them now. Two years before she had seen Yosef and Menashe sitting on a bench on the sidewalk, gossiping. Two old men, she laughs, one with a cane, and one with a walker. Six months ago she had received a message for Moshe about the death of his older brother, but she didn't pass it on and didn't take him to the funeral, because she didn't want the family to see him in his present condition—soon I would see for myself. A week ago she had asked Alex to drive past the stores; yes, it probably had to do with my visit. Memories started to surface once I accepted her invitation. In the past the stores had loomed large. Today she can see how rundown they are: their dirty windows, the sparse customers, most of whom can barely make ends meet.

"You don't feel connected to that anymore?" I am talking about myself, really, although I address the question to Adella.

Part of her is still down on her knees, she admits. Twenty years later that part continues to scrub the filthy bakery floor. And as for integrating the two segments of herself, joining the younger self to the current one that counts hundred-dollar bills in an elegant boutique, she has already given up on fitting them together. She has learned to allow them to exist in parallel, which is what happens to people whose lives are transformed in an instant.

"But my uncle is the connection between the two. He was with you during both parts, right?" The obvious mutual fondness that had been there from the start, her soft voice when she spoke to him during their first meeting—I had been a witness to that moment in Yarden's bedroom. Had that endured?

Yes, she had liked my Uncle Moshe right away. And to this day there has rarely been a harsh word between them. He has always been by her side, sometimes even opposing his siblings, but he is older than she and disabled. And for all these years she has made almost every decision by herself. And she had to fight battles with nearly all of his siblings from the very beginning.

"So why did you agree?" I try unsuccessfully to defend that young girl, drenched in the rain.

Because of the dream, says Adella as a shadow seems to cross her face. On the night when she turned eighteen her dead mother came to her in a dream—it had been years since she had come to her—and warned her against the suitor with the crowded mouth, who, as if he too had witnessed the dream, redoubled his efforts, and even after they found him a wife continued to think about Adella and phone her. Her mother told her that soon a potential husband would be suggested, and that she should accept the offer because he was her intended. And on the Friday of that very week she was approached by my Aunt Lily, who often came to the boarding school to bring food to her daughter, and she offered to introduce Adella to her younger brother as a marriage prospect.

"You know that wasn't really your mother who appeared in the dream, but your own desire?" I quote my psychologist.

Today she understands; she looks over at the revolving door across the street; she has learned a lot in her conversations with the owner of the store and with the customers. She falls silent, and I wonder. If she hadn't heeded her dream, if she had had a husband who was nothing but a burden to her for her entire life, if it hadn't been for my mother's relatives who trampled all over her and attacked her with some kind of baffling hostility, how high would the girl from the boarding school have soared? Is it a story about an opportunity almost missed that she wants me to write? Is there a success story here, or is it a story of a narrow escape?

Today it's easy for her to understand, she says, her eyes still focused on the door rotating on its axis. It's easier for strong people to rebel because they aren't risking their very existence. Today she's strong. Did she mention that she owns the store? Yes, yes. After years of flying back and forth to Germany, the owner decided to move there permanently to be close to her daughter and her grandchildren, one of whom suffered from an attention deficit disorder and had to be ferried to numerous appointments with specialists. And when he was a little older and there were fewer demands on her time, she opened a boutique, a kind of branch of this one, on a street of pretty shops in Munich, and Adella sends her sweaters to sell. Yes, a happy laugh escapes her, her accountant has her registered as an exporter. The boutique in Munich does very well, as does her store here in Tel Aviv. She is always amazed at the sums of money that women are willing to shell out for clothes. Sometimes, when she thinks back on her difficult years, it seems almost immoral to her to spend thousands of dollars on clothes rather than to help the girls who live in institutions. But that's the way of the world, and she has learned a lot about the psychology of women from her years of catering to them.

"Such as?" I'm curious.

"Such as, the unhappier a woman is, the less she will hesitate to spend more money." She smiles as though she has just revealed a deep secret, adding that usually it will be spent on an expensive garment that doesn't suit her and that she will probably never wear. Initially, after sales like those, her conscience would trouble her, and she decided that she would grant the women special permission to exchange the item they had purchased, and some of them, after riding out a wave of sadness, did return to replace it with something more practical. Even some of the best-educated women who shopped at her store didn't seem to understand that you can't heal misery with clothes; she smiles a melancholy smile for the sad nature of womankind. It's hard to believe what women are willing to do during their lowest moments. When she told my Uncle Moshe about these instances he found it hard to believe that women behaved in such a way, but how could he understand? He had no experience of women; she smiles at me now, and I try to surmise whether she is smiling bitterly, or with compassion.

"And when can I see Uncle Moshe?"

"Now." She gets to her feet, indicating to the waiter with a flourish of a hand signing her name in the air that he should add the cost of our refreshments to her bill and turns to leave.

For most of the short distance between the hotel and her home on Ben Yehuda Street we walk arm in arm as Adella prepares me to meet my Uncle Moshe.

My heart sinks at her descriptions, delivered fluently in a lighthearted tone. The most beloved of my uncles seems to be approaching the end of his life. Is this why she asked me to come? When she has finished explaining we walk in silence the rest of the way.

To my relief, my uncle is sitting in a wheelchair. Standing at his side is a Filipino carer speaking on his phone in English. I look around as Adella looks at me, viewing the apartment through my gaze.

The first sight that meets the eye is that of the sea, stretched out along the beach and extending to the horizon. Very blue and very wide and very near, almost grazing the window. I feel like reaching out to touch it. The kitchen and living area are one large, clean space where everything is in its place. The apartment is sparsely furnished, almost monkish, yet comfortable.

Despite having been prepared by Adella, my heart isn't ready yet for this meeting with the pale man in his wheelchair, his head listing to one side with saliva shining at the corner of his mouth. The stern-faced Filipino wipes it away from time to time.

"Do you remember Micha, your sister Michal's son?" She talks to him like I talked to the twins when they were a couple of weeks old, and I wonder if it bothers him, because he swings his head from side to side like an old lion. I am surprised to see that some of his good looks remain in the sick man in the wheelchair, as I note the slope of his shoulders, the thick mane of hair, which is now completely white. But his eyes put me in mind of the gaze of his sister across the ocean: opaque, looking through me, with not a flicker of recognition. His mouth, as though the eyes and the lips are not connected to each other, is curved in a permanent smile. It seems I was mistaken, because now Adella is speaking to him in an ordinary way, as though she is unaware of the state he is in, and for a moment she seems to me like an actress on a stage. "Do you remember Micha? He arrived yesterday from Los Angeles. Do you know where he's staying? On the seventh floor in room seven hundred and seventeen. Of course you remember, that was our honeymoon room, you remember that room very well."

I gape amazed at the theater unfolding before my eyes. Is this performance intended for me or for my uncle? All at once I revert to being the child surrounded by his cousins who are like no other people in the whole wide world. How was their existence forgotten during the time when I was in Los Angeles, how were the priorities overturned, so that first place was now occupied by the fact that I was American, speaking English so fluently that the language was an inseparable part of me, part of my profession, part of the woman I chose to live with until she packed my bags and ordered me to leave?

But here I am Micha the child again, the designated bridesman, and I kneel before my Uncle Moshe, look directly into his frozen pupils, and stroke the fingers resting motionlessly in his lap, remember those fingers constantly trembling, and see that, now that they have finally used up their ration of tremors, they lie still, and with that caress I convey to him my love which was dormant within me but hasn't diminished at all in the years we haven't seen each other.

From my position on the floor I see a familiar face in a photograph visible above my uncle's shoulder. It takes me a moment to understand from the Che Guevara print on the T-shirt that it isn't a picture of me in my youth, but a picture of Elisha. Later I realize that it's one of the series of photos that Adella showed me earlier on her phone. I turn to Adella, searching for an answer in her eyes, and find them full of tears. I approach the picture, pick it up and study it, but she snatches it from my hands and returns it to its place, as if her entire purpose is to make sure that things are undisturbed. And the whole time my uncle is watching us both, as if he doesn't understand a thing, and I suspect that he understands everything.

Suddenly I want to run for my life, to get away from here without stopping at the hotel, without a word of farewell, to sprint all the way to the airport and straight onto the plane and, as if nothing has happened, to land softly back in my familiar life. To return to my wife and the twins and my work, to forget the terrible period when I lived without them, to forget about this invitation to come to Israel, which for good reason I haven't visited since I left, as if I sensed that doing so could lead to nothing good.

But I'm still here, facing my uncle's hollow stare, facing Adella's tearful eyes.

Aware of my strong resemblance to my uncle, I observe him as though I have been granted an opportunity to catch a glimpse of my future self. If I am spared the wheelchair and the immobile face, if I manage to hold up my head and not to drool, I could be an impressive looking venerable sixty-eight-year-old. I angle my head so that it is facing his, which droops on his neck, and look into his eyes, probing for a spark of life, of acknowledgement, with my peripheral vision seeking the slightest movement in the lips stretched in their perpetual grin.

"Goodbye Uncle Moshe." I lean down and speak the words almost directly into his ear. "It's Micha, Adella's bridesman from your wedding, the one who came to your house so sick before he left for America, your nephew, the son of your sister Michal, how are you doing?"

If I hadn't known that his smile was really a spasm, I could have credited it with some kind of insight, as a wise, wry smile at the vanities of the world. Suddenly he exerts pressure on one of my fingers, and I am overcome. "Do you know me, Uncle Moshe? Do you remember your sister Michal? I'm her son."

But it appears that this touch of his hand is another kind of twitch. His eyes are devoid of expression. What is going on behind that attractive brow?

Adella searches frantically through her purse, finds a tissue to wipe her eyes, and, clutching her bag, blocks my path to the photograph. She speaks to me, brandishing her phone, and some time passes before I realize what she's saying, she's sorry, she thought it would take her four days to tell me her story, but it seems that she has completed the task in two. She has related the story in full, and I am free to use it as I like. But from here on in she won't be able to spend any more time with me, because today—and again she waves her phone in my direction—this very day an urgent and unexpected order is arriving and she can't be away from her studio. And as I can see, my Uncle Moshe can't be of any help to me either. She is sorry now that she persuaded me to stay for four days when I myself had asked to come for only two. So she is sure that I will be glad to know that right now, this very minute, she will change my flight, and with her agent it won't be any problem at all. There's always room in Business Class. It's five o'clock, and there's a flight at midnight. Alex will pick me up in front of the hotel at nine, so I have time to get organized and pack. Can I find my way back to the hotel without her? From the entrance to the house I should turn right onto Frishman Street and then right again onto Hayarkon.

My uncle doesn't understand a thing. He looks at me like a child.

"It's true that I only wanted to come for two days, but you insisted on four, so I cleared my schedule. And I had hoped that I would be able to see Elisha—" I have no idea why I'm arguing with her, since she has read my mind and granted me my wish to go straight back home.

No, no. She already told me that I can't meet Elisha. He's studying for exams and he mustn't be disturbed, and now he has a girlfriend—

"And I had planned to visit my grandfather's grave . . ." I tell her.

She'll never manage to find his grave. Since the funeral, dozens of years ago, she hasn't been to the cemetery, and there's no one left to ask. Now, she clears her throat to forge a path through the tears threatening to choke her, now she really must ask me to return to the hotel and get ready. If I need any more details about the story of her life, we can speak on the phone, or even Skype; yes, yes, she knows how to use Skype.

"Micha is going now." She leans over Uncle Moshe, "He has to get back to Los Angeles today, say goodbye to Micha."

Uncle Moshe is confused. I part from him with a squeeze of his paralyzed fingers, extending my own so that they wrap around his hand, hoping he may discern my touch. Slowly Adella pulls me away by the arm, and with a hug, which turns out to be her farewell embrace, she gently pushes me out the door, but I defy her and push back, hold it open, because I have an urgent question.

"So why, why did you ask me to come? Why now?" I whisper what demands to be asked.

I won't believe it, she tells me through the narrowing gap in the door, but she thought that I was still Persian and Israeli, although now she realizes how American I have become, and over there they excel at logic, and maybe after all this time I am just like them. Maybe the heart that offered her the almonds when I was nine years old has vanished in America, but maybe in the future I will manage to open that heart, when I stop to think about things, maybe that heart will come out of hiding to fulfil its dreams. Her mother came to her in a dream and told her to invite me to come. Yes, yes. It's true that her mother never really knew me, but her mother has been with her all her life, directing her to the right places—she shuts the door, and the final sliver of space between us is gone.

Once again I'm in Business Class, this time flying westward, and once again I am thinking about the mystery of Adella's invitation as I ponder my sudden departure and realize that, although she didn't tell me in so many words, I was not summoned to document the years Adella spent at the boarding school nor the years that preceded them. I am the witness to her transformation. When I left at age fifteen she had reached the nadir of her life, and it was clearly important to her that I know that she had risen from rock bottom entirely on her own and become a respected and affluent woman. Maybe she had invited me so that through me she could denounce my aunts and uncles, some of whom were dead, for the injustice they had done her in her youth, and certainly to display her fabulous success. Yes, I am sure. Her story is no less worthy of a book than are those of the famous people to whom I provide the service of a ghostwriter.

And still reflecting on Adella's story, perhaps under the influence of the free drinks being served, I fall asleep in my comfortable seat, and in my dream a fire ignites in my body, which wakes me, and I remember where I am and sit up with a jolt. I recall feeling the same internal burning during that final exam, and the memory evokes a chain of sensations which followed the distant conflagration—the smell of the interior of the gym teacher's car; the feeling of falling backward into space; the comfort of the firm mattress; the scent of the skin of a woman who sits beside me and wipes my brow sometimes with a damp cloth and sometimes with the palm of her hand.

Suddenly I see the face of Adella from years ago coming close to mine, and I feel my young body raging with fever and her soft fingers travelling along the nape of my neck, trailing pinpricks of heat, and the sensation of another body pressing into the length of my body, a trembling so intense that my teeth chatter, the electric shock of hot lips meeting mine. I jerk forward in my seat, and the air hostess rushes to my side. "Is everything all right, sir?"

My face is red-hot, and for a crazy moment I feel as though the heat in my body is melting my eyes in their sockets. The stewardess brings me a cup of water, and I drink it down in one gulp, to extinguish the fire.

What is this forgotten memory bursting forth? I try to marshal my thoughts, realizing that it is my mother's description of the events rather than my own memories that I have relied on for all these years to describe what actually happened from the minute the gym teacher brought me like a mother carrying her child from the car to the bed at Adella's house until I saw my father and my brother and my sister Yarden waving and smiling, waiting for us, excited, at the airport in Los Angeles.

A short time later, staring out the window at the cloud clusters bunching together like piles of fluffy cotton candy, the suspicion buds and blooms. Under cover of the raging fever that rendered me semi-conscious, Adella slipped into my bed, availed herself of my young male body's obliging virility, and got herself pregnant. A demonic whirl of images, scents, and impressions assails me. Her lips approaching mine, the grinding of body against body, arms holding me, a surging, ascending heat and release, the scent of her in my nostrils. If not—now I'm thinking coolly, dispassionately—why hadn't she become pregnant during the five years following her wedding, and not in all the subsequent years; but a short time after I landed in Los Angeles, only then, we heard the news that she was pregnant.

Gazing out terrified at the sky I think, Adella was impregnated by me twenty-four years ago. She had hinted as much in every possible way. That's why she said it was I who had rescued her from a life of slavery, meaning through the child I gave her. Was that why her voice shook when she asked what I recalled from the time when I was sick and how I had learned that she was pregnant? Was that why she insisted, despite the awkwardness, on providing me with details about her sex life with my uncle? Was the pretext about writing her story invented to parade her changed status or in an attempt to ascertain whether I could handle the revelation that we two had a child? Had she brought me to her home to meet my Uncle Moshe so I could see for myself that he didn't have long to live? Had she, in fact, heard the rumor of my separation from my wife? Had she invited me to see with her own eyes how I would react, to gauge whether I would agree—when I realized that I was the father of her child—to come and take the place of my uncle in her life? Could it be that when she realized that my life—with or without my wife—was firmly anchored on the other side of the ocean she sought to punish me and that's why she grabbed the picture of Elisha from my hands and wouldn't allow me to meet him? Is that why she cut short my visit and packed me off, back to Los Angeles? Is it possible that my mother caught her in the act with my fifteen-year-old self, lying feverish and semi-conscious in bed at her house and that was the reason for their final argument? Did my Uncle Moshe know about it? Is that why she suddenly stopped talking when we were sitting in the café? Is that why she held back when telling me her story? What happened to her in the moment when I met my Uncle Moshe? Does Elisha know? Is that why she suddenly seemed afraid? Was the invitation somehow connected to the girl Elisha might marry? Did Adella want Elisha's birth father to be part of that momentous occasion?

A sweet feeling rocks my being. So I had lost my virginity to Adella. I would have to rewrite my sexual history.

If I had been at the wheel of a car, with a squealing of tires I would have made an abrupt U-turn to go back and confirm my hypotheses. A seeming cliché uttered by Adella takes on profound meaning: "Things aren't always what they seem," as if she had provided me with the answer before I knew there was a question.

It was at that moment that the realization hit me. Adella wanted to give me something in return. She had referred to the fact that I was a ghostwriter. She might have read the online interviews with me, some of which include the names of impressive clients who had granted me permission to publish them. She had just reminded me that the first time we met, when I was nine, I had told her that I wanted to be a writer, and here I was, grazing forty, and I still hadn't written a book of my own. Was she granting me the gift of this story to help me emerge from the shadows into the light?

And I knew I wouldn't tell my wife or anyone else, just as Adella hadn't told my uncle or Elisha. The secret would be buried with the two of us. It seemed she had tried to hint as much to me, and then changed her mind.

I close my eyes and begin to retell myself Adella's story according to the sequence of events that begins on the day she was born and ends when she pushes me out the door of her apartment on Ben Yehuda Street. There are still many details to be deciphered from within the narrative, and I mark them in my memory.

When I went back to the hotel room to pack my things, I found a parcel sitting on the bed containing two beautiful sweaters encased in silk wrapping, one for my mother and one for my wife, I imagined. Underneath it rested a thick notebook and next to it a pen, displayed like a jewel in a decorative wooden case. And inside the case I found a folded note, written in the familiar hand that had filled that ancient notebook in the wondrous suitcase of fabrics: "May this notebook mark the beginning of the realization of a dream."

Standing motionless, I observed the gifts, wondering when they were placed on my bed. It had to have been before I visited my uncle, before I asked to meet Elisha, before my sudden banishment. Was this a coincidence, or was it all part of a carefully crafted plan?

And maybe, I add this part now, as I plunge my hand into my bag in search of the wooden box, maybe in this way Adella is repaying the debt of the sugared almonds and providing me with a lesson learned by someone who came into this world with no assets beyond her dreams, went to war on her own, limping and nearsighted, and with her own hands built a family, a home, and a livelihood. Maybe this is a metaphor for the riddle of the world which moves in circles, where objects spin eternally around the axis of the universe, and in this way my generosity of spirit at age nine is rewarded now with the ingredients of a story.

A vision forms itself before my eyes. When writing the memoirs of others I always augment the process with family photographs provided by my clients to flesh out the people and places they have told me about. I pin them to a corkboard facing my computer and consult them as necessary. Never before had an image emerged so clearly and brightly lit from the very depths of my body, more real than reality, with all its miniscule components plain to see. And none of the photographs I had ever received were as multi-dimensional as the picture which floated up behind my closed eyelids, revealing to me a young girl sitting deep inside a green armchair, her hair wet, the lenses of her glasses thick. Wind-whipped raindrops pelt the window behind her. I direct my eyes to the fabric of the chair and see velvet the color of green grass, threaded with tiny dots of dust trapped in the fibers in arched squiggles left in the grooves by the bristles of the cleaning brush. Shifting my gaze to the window I see the jets of water illuminated by the light shining from the adjacent balcony, streaming in diagonal lines in the headlights, exploding against the windshields and leaving splinters of water in their wake, spraying like tiny fountains. I focus my gaze on the girl and note her heart-shaped mouth, her bulky glasses threatening to sink into the bridge of her nose, the quick, troubled look in her eyes, blurred behind the thick lenses.

I'm not sure at exactly which point above the ocean I decided to rummage in my bag to find Adella's parting gift to me; maybe it was when the plane flew over the Bermuda Triangle. The childhood I had separated from in one wrenching movement, which I buried too early so that it wouldn't obstruct being swallowed up by America, that same childhood that had refused to go and lingered in deep shadows, sent a tremor of restlessness into my new reality.

For the remainder of the flight to Los Angeles I bear astonished witness to images that spring to life, oscillating between heaven and earth, my body and my mind and my memories and my imagination coming together in an alliance of words, each of which is the right word and describes precisely what my eyes are seeing, and every word glows in its sentence, like a precious gem set in the exact position where every one of its facets sparkles and gleams in the perfect light at the correct angle, and as I reconstruct the wonder of creation, I write,

I met her for the first time on a Saturday evening in the winter that would be recorded as the rainiest of the decade. She sat on the green velvet armchair in my grandfather's spacious living room, folded deep into its recesses as though seeking shelter from the many pairs of prying eyes boring into her . . .

About the Author

Savyon Liebrecht was born in Munich in
1948 to Holocaust survivors who immigrated
to Israel soon afterwards. She studied philos-
ophy and literature at Tel Aviv University and
began her writing career in 1986. She has received several awards for her work, including
the Alterman Prize and the Amelia Rosselli
Prize, and has been named Israel's Playwright
of the Year twice. Her books have been translated into nine languages. She lives in Tel Aviv.